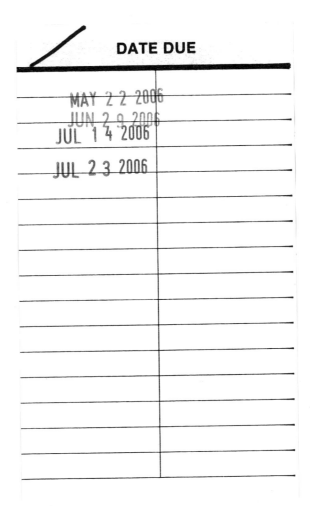

DATE DUE

THE YING
ON TRIAD

A
Tony Boudreaux
Mystery

THE YING
ON TRIAD

A Tony Boudreaux Mystery

•

Kent Conwell

AVALON BOOKS
NEW YORK

Published by Thomas Bouregy & Co., Inc.
160 Madison Avenue, New York, NY 10016

Library of Congress Cataloging-in-Publication Data

Conwell, Kent.
    The ying on triad / Kent Conwell.
        p. cm.
    ISBN 0-8034-9758-X (acid-free paper)
    1. Triads (Gangs)—Fiction. 2. Suspense fiction. I. Title.

PS3553.O547Y56 2006
813'.54—dc22

                                            2005028542

PRINTED IN THE UNITED STATES OF AMERICA
ON ACID-FREE PAPER
BY HADDON CRAFTSMEN, BLOOMSBURG, PENNSYLVANIA

To Susan—who doesn't know the meaning of quit.

Chapter One

Now everyone knows a corpse can't talk, especially one that has been dead ten years. But in seven harrowing days, I discovered there is more than one way to talk. Red Tompkins proved it to me. And in so doing, he reminded me that fate directs our lives with both a trace of humor and a handful of mockery.

Over the years I've made fair progress at Blevins' Investigations, rising from the more plebeian jobs of running down skips and tailing errant husbands or wives to the more substantial work of S & L scams, personnel background searches, and even turning up evidence to help the local law collar a killer or two. It wasn't the kind of excitement that would entice James Bond to leave the French Rivera, but for a country boy from Church Point, Louisiana, it was satisfying.

However, somewhere along the way I had forgotten the sobering truth that life gets its kicks from throwing curveballs; and this time the pitch coming at me had as wicked a break as any I had ever faced.

To make matters worse I had only one strike, and if I swung and missed, Bobby Packard would be out of the game of life. The state of Texas would see to that. Final score, Texas–1; Bobby Packard–0.

That pitch lasted seven days, seven interminable days that were a potpourri made up of a significant other who wanted to play detective; an ex-wife showing up in town; a millionaire friend soliciting my help to run for city hall; the sudden, but not surprising appearance of my old man who had stolen my laptop at the last family reunion; a testy mob underboss; secretive Asian tongs and triads; and a corpse that had vanished.

In other words, fate had decided it was time for my handful of mockery.

October weather in Central Texas is a celebration of fickleness. If Mother Nature isn't satisfied in the morning, she'll make changes by afternoon. In my years around Austin, I've seen ninety degrees one day and snow the next. In Texas, the credibility of weather prognostication is right up there with fortune-telling.

The day that Danny O'Banion, Austin's rumored *caporegime*, walked into Blevins' Investigations was chilly and quiet, and his appearance made the day grow even quieter. Two of my co-workers abruptly stopped their conversation and stared at Danny in astonishment.

Standing in the open doorway with his oversized bodyguard, Huey—aka Godzilla—behind him, Danny calmly surveyed the office. When he spotted me, he smiled faintly and nodded, his freckled face and tousled red hair reminding me of a modern-day Tom Sawyer. "Hello, Tony," he said, striding across the room to my desk and holding out his hand.

Danny and I have a history, and I was always glad to see him despite the fact that he was connected big-time to the mob. I shook his hand. "Hey, Danny. What's up?" I gestured to a chair at the side of my desk.

He slipped into the chair. Huey stood towering over him.

"Hello, Huey," I said, nodding at the big man. The first time I had seen Huey was at night on a narrow road west of Austin. His square face had looked like a chunk of chipped granite, square and solid, with no distinguishing features other than a couple fissures for eyes, a square knob for a nose, and a third crevice that was probably his mouth. It hadn't changed over the years.

Huey grunted.

For him, a single grunt was considered garrulous. Still, I owed him. Two years earlier he had saved my life out at the Chalk Hills Distillery by taking a slug meant for me.

"Well, Danny, what brings you down here? Slumming?"

He glanced over my shoulder. I looked around. My boss, Marty Blevins, stood gaping at us through the window of his office door. "That's Marty," I explained. "My boss."

I hesitated, puzzled by Danny's sudden appearance. He seldom left his lair on the top floor of the Green Light Parking Garage in downtown Austin. Whatever had brought him out must be important.

Leaning back in his chair, Danny crossed one leg over the other and drew a deep breath. "Tony, I need your help." He nodded to Marty who, with no hint of shame, continued to stare out the window at us. "Maybe I should say, I need your company's help."

For a moment, I thought I had misunderstood him. "*Our* help? You mean you want to hire us?" I had always been a fast thinker.

With a terse nod he explained, "I have a cousin on death row in Huntsville for the murder of Albert Hastings ten or eleven years ago. Hastings was the governor-elect at that time."

Nodding slowly, I vaguely remembered the headlines shouting about the murder.

Danny continued, "Bobby is scheduled for lethal injection on November 4, seven days from now. I want you to find the real killer before then."

I frowned.

"Just after Bobby's arrest, our uncle, Liam McCulloch, claimed a man by the name of Red tried to sell him a video showing who had really killed Hastings. This Red claimed the shooter was a Chink," he shrugged, "—maybe connected to a triad."

I just stared at Danny. His surprising request had overloaded my brain, and for a moment, both hemispheres of that puny organ threatened to shut down like my old computer. Finally, the gray matter rebooted itself, but all I could do was blink like the innocuous cursor.

A faint smile flickered over his lips. "This is strictly legit, Tony. My people aren't part of it. This is family."

Hesitantly, I replied, "None of—ah, no one—huh? Just you?"

"And a couple uncles and aunts—family. You know, personal family. Not business family."

I was still having trouble absorbing his request. "You have more connections than we do, Danny. Why don't you find this Red? Can't your uncle help?"

His eyes narrowed, and a wry smile ticked up one side of his lips. "First, Uncle Liam's dead. His heart . . . five years ago.

And we looked for this Red guy, but he dropped out of sight. I could have put out the word, but the ones I work for were very upset about the governor-elect's death." He paused, the wry grin on his lips turning down. "Let's just say that because of business ramifications, they wouldn't be interested in freeing the man convicted of killing that particular governor-elect."

After digesting his words a few moments, I understood what he hadn't said. Pushing back from the desk, I motioned for him to accompany me. "We need to talk to my boss about this, Danny," I said, leading the way to Marty's office. "There are a couple of . . . well . . . unusual sides to this job."

He chuckled, "I'd say more than a couple."

Marty hastily backed away from the door when he saw us coming in his direction. His bulging eyes shifted rapidly from Danny to Huey, ignoring me.

I opened the door and gestured for Danny and Huey to enter. "Marty, you know Danny O'Banion. And this is Huey."

Marty's fleshy forehead glistened with perspiration. He nodded once, then dragged the tip of his tongue across his lips. "Ah . . . well, not personally," he stammered. "I— I've seen your picture in the papers, Mr. O'Banion. Please, have . . . have a seat," he stuttered, indicating the chairs in front of his desk and rubbing at the sweaty rolls of fat around his size twenty-two neck. "Nice pictures," he added hastily.

Huey, as expected, remained standing. I took the second chair and explained, "Marty, ten years ago Danny's cousin went to prison convicted of the murder of Albert Hastings, the governor-elect at the time. Danny wants to hire us to prove his cousin is innocent of the murder. His uncle claimed someone tried to sell him film showing the real killer."

Marty stared at me, expecting more.

I shrugged. "That's it. And, oh yeah, the uncle's dead now." I waited, watching the wheels turn in Marty's head.

Danny spoke up. "Look, Marty, it's like I told Tony. This is personal, not *business*," he said, emphasizing the word business. He paused, studying Marty to see if he grasped Danny's meaning.

Marty's forehead wrinkled. "Personal? Not business? You mean, it has nothing to do with—"

Danny cut him off. "I mean, it's personal. My cousin is on death row for a murder he says he didn't commit. We found out today his last appeal was denied. That's why I didn't come to Tony sooner," he grimaced, "which could prove to be a mistake on my part."

"It happened about ten years ago, Marty," I explained. "Remember the guy who shot the governor-elect?"

Marty frowned, then his eyes widened in surprise. "That's him? That's your cousin?"

Danny nodded.

"He has a week, Marty," I put in. "Next week—November 4—is the date of execution."

Marty was greedy, but also worried about his company's reputation, about crossing the mob, and about offending the local law. Through his beady eyes, I could read the thoughts whirling in his frenetic little brain. What if city hall objected? They could pull strings to create all sorts of problems for a company. The local law agencies might stop being so helpful. They might take away his free parking downtown. "I don't know, Mr. O'Banion. We're booked up pretty solid around here."

Danny glanced up at me and winked. His blue eyes gleamed with amusement. "Tell you what, Marty. I'll pay you twenty-five hundred a day and if you keep Bobby from the needle, a ten thousand dollar bonus."

That was all Marty needed to forget his company's reputation, the mob, city hall, and downtown parking. He looked up at me with a concerned expression on his face. "I know you have a big workload, Tony, but I think we should do all we can to help Mr. O'Banion. After all, we are talking about an innocent man here. We need to do what we can, don't you think?" He turned away from me and gave Danny a beaming, beneficent smile.

The grin that played across Danny's freckled face told me what I already knew, that he read Marty like a book, which wasn't hard since Marty possessed the mentality of an elementary schoolboy.

"Yeah, Marty," I replied, trying to keep the sarcasm from my tone. "That would be the Christian thing to do."

Keeping his eyes on Danny and completely oblivious to my sarcasm, he replied, "I think so too. I really do."

One side of Danny's lips curled.

Even Huey snorted.

I glanced at him. The crevice on his face that his was mouth appeared to quiver.

Marty looked at me. "Tell you what, Tony. Tomorrow, you drive up to Huntsville and visit with . . . ah . . ."

"Robert Packard," Danny said.

"Yeah, Robert Packard. You need to get up there and see him."

I frowned. "What about visiting hours? I didn't think that on death row—"

"Don't worry about that," Danny assured me. "They'll let you in whenever you arrive."

My frown deepened.

He winked at me. "Trust me. You won't run into any problems up there. I'll take care of it for you."

"Okay with me," I replied. If Danny said things were taken care of, then they were. I knew from experience.

Marty cleared his throat. "And, Tony."

I looked around at him. "Yeah?"

"When you get back from Huntsville, go over the interview with Nathan Savage. We don't have much time."

Danny gave me a curious look.

Savage? I bit my tongue. In what I hoped was a calm, firm voice, I said, "I don't need Savage, Marty. I can handle this myself."

He looked around at me, momentarily puzzled, and then a broad grin split his pan-shaped face. "Sure you can, Tony, sure you can. But Nathan's got thirteen years' experience.

Bounce it off him, and he might have an idea or two. A different slant. All right?"

With a deep sigh, I replied, "All right. I'll need a transcript of the trial."

"I'll have it to you first thing in the morning." Danny snapped his fingers, and Huey grunted.

"Early. I'm leaving for Huntsville at six."

"It'll be at your place before five-thirty."

I reached for the phone. I never interfered with police business. I figured Austin P.D. had no interest in Bobby Packard, but I called Chief Ramon Pachuca, a third-generation Hispanic, for his blessing, which he gave.

Nodding to Marty and Danny, I said, "Let's get on with it."

Marty grinned up at me. "And make me proud."

I clenched my teeth. That was his departing remark to everyone. *Make me proud.* Like a father. I often wondered if he said it to his son when the boy took the throne in the bathroom. *Make me proud, son.*

Chapter Two

Venturing into Austin traffic five years ago was a challenge; today, it was a decided risk. Horrendous, hideous, and horrific most aptly describe the daily dash from home to work and back again. At any given time, thousands of automobiles jam the freeways bumper-to-bumper two miles in every direction from downtown.

The daredevil attempt to take an on-ramp into the middle of the melee of motorcycles, cars, pickups, and trucks is not for the faint-hearted. Such an attempt demands that a driver possess supreme confidence, consummate skill, and a death wish.

Every time I manage to shoehorn my Silverado pickup into traffic, I'm truly amazed. The drawback is that once in the middle, you're going where the others go. Changing lanes is not unlike Russian roulette with five cartridges in the cylinder.

When I hit I-35 North that afternoon, my brain was replaying the conversation with Danny. So involved was I that out of habit I took the off-ramp to my old apartment on Travis, except I no longer lived on Travis.

Muttering a curse, I sped along the access road until I

reached the next on-ramp, where I once again tempted fate. Two miles north, I managed the appropriate cutoff to Gin Peyton Road and my new apartment. The move had been prompted by the need to garage my newest toy, a 1925 Model T Runabout that I'd picked up over in Mississippi while helping Jack Edney find the person who had killed his father.

Unfortunately, the perp turned out to be Jack's sister, who managed to escape the proverbial long arm of the law; but Joe Basco, a mob boss in New Orleans, had a longer arm that had stretched from the French Quarter to a deserted road in the middle of the swamp twenty miles south of Vicksburg.

Jack's old man had restored Model T's and T-birds. I fell in love with the Runabout and bought it for fifteen thousand. In the process of the investigation in Vicksburg, my 2002 Silverado pickup was literally ripped apart, and Jack, who came into almost six million dollars—most of it because of me—replaced it with a new one.

So, I had hooked a lowboy trailer to the new Silverado, driven the Runabout up onto it, and headed home.

Janice Coffman-Morrison, my significant other, fell in love with the little antique just as I knew she would— despite the fact she routinely sold her own vehicles when they were six months old or needed washing, whichever came first. In the last few months, we had put a few hundred miles on it just tooling around town at a breakneck thirty miles per hour.

The red light on the answering machine was blinking when I entered the apartment. I punched the button and headed to the bedroom to change. There were two messages, the first was Janice reminding me of our dinner date that night at the Hilton Towers, a spectacular restaurant overlooking the broad Colorado River, and the second, a voice like gravel, warning me, "Leave Packard where he is."

I glanced at the caller ID. The source was unavailable. I punched in *69, then dialed the number and was rewarded with a recording saying the number was out of service. Probably a pay phone, I guessed. I studied the receiver in my hand for several seconds before replacing it. Whoever was responsible for the call was clever. There was no way to trace a pay phone to an individual.

While I was dressing the phone rang. It was Janice. "Did you get my message?"

"I'm almost ready."

"Oh, and," she exclaimed, "I forgot to mention something. Don't plan anything for Sunday. Aunt Beatrice is giving a small party out at the distillery. If the weather is pretty, we can drive out in the little car."

Little car. That was the tender sobriquet she had given the Model T Runabout. "Fine with me if I have the time."

"Tony!"

"I'm serious, Janice. I'm working on a new case, and I'm pressed for time."

"Well," she sniffed, "certainly not so pressed you can't take off an hour or so for me."

An hour or so? More like three or four hours. "We'll see."

As usual, I drove over to her apartment where I left my Silverado so we could go in her two-month-old silver Miata. She didn't truly dislike my pickup, but she did have an aversion to being seen in it by any of her friends from the Daylily Club or any of the several other social organizations to which she belonged.

"You look wonderful," I said, climbing from the truck and sliding behind the wheel of the silver Miata. "Have you been waiting long?"

She smiled briefly from the passenger seat. "I had just closed the door."

I leaned over and touched my lips to hers. "Ready?"

She nodded.

Before I shifted gears, I caught a puzzling glimpse of her. She seemed distracted. "Are you all right?"

I know that's not the question a smart man should ask a woman who seems to have something on her mind, but I didn't know what else to say.

Her answer told me something was bothering her. "Fine. I'm just fine."

I played the dummy. "Good. Let's go." I gunned the engine, and the little Miata leaped forward.

Janice and I had met a few years earlier when I was helping her out of an insurance jam. Neither she nor I were interested in getting serious, but we had fun together even though I quickly realized I was simply a dependable escort, an infrequent lover, an occasional confidant.

In other words, I was a tool to satisfy her needs. And she was the same for me. We had reconciled our positions in the relationship and we were both fairly content.

Inexplicably, despite our skewed relationship, we were very good friends who enjoyed each other's company. From time to time, Janice did speak of *our relationship*. After a few of those little discussions, which I really didn't understand, I learned when to agree and when not to agree.

That night, Janice was a knockout with diamonds draped around her slender neck and dangling from her ears. There's an ethereal quality about the very rich that the rest of us never quite manage to successfully emulate.

As always, we enjoyed each other during an evening of elegant dining and dancing despite her occasional inattentiveness. I kept up an innocuous chitchat through-out the evening, but for some reason, she seemed to maintain an inexplicable distance. Which prompted me to begin wondering what I had done wrong.

Just before midnight, she cleared her throat. "Tony, we need to talk."

Talk! I cringed. Beware when a woman says you need to talk. Warily, I replied with a response I knew couldn't get me in trouble, "Oh?" My brain raced, wondering what was coming next.

With a tender and gentle smile, she laid her hand on mine. "I can't tell you how wonderful the last few months have been, since you came back from Vicksburg."

I relaxed—not much, but some. "Good," I choked out, still wary, still wondering.

"I feel we're closer now than we've ever been, don't you?" she squeezed my hand.

Relaxing a little more, I squeezed hers back. "I was beginning to wonder. You've seemed, well, distracted to-night."

A becoming blush tinged her cheeks, and she ducked her head. "That's because . . . well, I wanted to talk to you about something, and I didn't know how you would react."

I squeezed her hand again and replied with the safest response I could muster. "You know you can talk to me about anything, Janice. Anything at all."

She looked up hopefully, "Anything?"

With smug grin, I nodded to her, "Anything."

Her eyes lit with glee. "I've been thinking about it, but this afternoon when you mentioned you might have to work Sunday, I made up my mind. I want to work with you, Tony. I want to help you investigate whatever it is you investigate. We'll make a wonderful team."

I laughed. Suddenly the laughter stuck in my throat

when I realized exactly what she had said. Maybe I had misunderstood. Nervously, I asked. "You—you . . . ah . . . what?"

Janice nodded emphatically. "I want to be your partner. I want to help you solve crimes like Nick and Nora Charles."

"Nick and Nora who? What on earth are you talking about?"

"You know," she said, her words gushing with excitement, "those two actors in the old movies back when talking films were just beginning. Way back in the olden days. I don't remember their real names, but they were on TV last week. Together they solved a big crime. That's what gave me the idea."

Now, I have always considered myself fairly glib. I taught English to high school kids who didn't want to learn, in schools that didn't want me to teach. And later, I did well selling insurance, but I was now at a loss for words. Janice was obviously enthralled with the idea, as she was with her many impulses. Most of them died a slow, agonizing death, and within a few weeks she usually found another interest.

Being heiress to the largest distillery in the state of Texas provides the luxury of indulging such caprices.

I enjoyed our time together. I didn't want an argument and the last thing I wanted her to do was start pouting. She was the ultimate pouter, probably having majored in pouting at the exclusive finishing school she had attended in Atlanta. The intensity of her pouting could make a firm decision suddenly limp.

Figuring this idea was simply a passing fancy, I tried to sidestep her suggestion. "It isn't what you think, Janice. There's nothing glamorous about the job."

Her brows knitted in an attractive frown. "Oh, I know

that. I know it's hard, but we can do it." She paused, then added, "Don't you think so?"

I whistled to myself. What a loaded question. I was sunk either way I answered, so I opted for the coward's way, "I sure do."

She jumped from her chair, clapping her hands in glee, and then she threw her arms around my neck, "Oh, Tony, thank you, thank you, thank you!"

Embarrassed by the puzzled frowns that quickly turned into beaming smiles from the tables around us, I hugged her to me. "All right, if you're going to work with me, I'd better get you home. I leave for death row in Huntsville at 6:00 in the morning."

She looked up in surprise and parted her lips to protest.

I quickly explained. "The job doesn't work on your hours. You have to go whenever and wherever the job calls, in all kinds of weather." It might have been a little melo-dramatic, but I was hoping she would change her mind.

She didn't. Instead, she pulled away and grabbed her wrap and purse. "Then take me home."

At 5:30 next morning, Huey delivered the transcript of the trial. I eyed it anxiously, eager to peruse the sheath of documents. I tossed it on the computer table so I would not forget to take it with me, after which I gave Oscar, my albino tiger barb, his morning feast. "Take it easy, little fella," I muttered, watching him as he swam in circles to suck the food from the surface of the aquarium.

To my surprise, Janice was waiting on the sidewalk when I pulled up in front of her apartment at 6 A.M. She wore a brown suit and a matching brown Dolce and Gabbana belted cardigan vest over a white silk blouse. *The perfect outfit for detecting*, I thought wryly.

At 9:00 A.M., we pulled up in front of the Polunsky Unit east of Livingston, Texas, forty miles or so southeast of Huntsville. I climbed out and glanced across the seat at Janice, "Well, are you ready?"

With grim apprehension, she eyed the bleak buildings surrounded by twelve-foot chain link fences topped with curls of concertina razor wire. She looked at me and shivered. "You go in. I'll wait out here."

I suppressed a grin. "I thought you wanted to be part of it—to work with me."

She drew a deep breath but her face had paled. "I do, but, but—this . . ." she gestured to the cold, severe buildings housing the death row inmates. "I'll wait for you out here."

Chapter Three

I don't know how Danny O'Banion had managed, but I ran into no problems in seeing Robert Packard. I was escorted into a small room with a single chair in front of a window looking into an adjoining room, which also contained only a single chair. On the wall beside the window, on each side, was a telephone receiver.

A few minutes later, a thin, dark-haired man with a sallow complexion entered. The door closed behind him. When he saw me, he frowned. I picked up the receiver. He followed my lead. "Bobby? I'm Tony Boudreaux. Your cousin, Danny O'Banion, sent me. He wants me to do what I can to help you."

Bobby arched an eyebrow. "Cutting the time short, isn't he?" Resentment edged his words.

"He acted as soon as he learned your appeal had been denied." I paused, he shrugged, and I continued, "Now, let's start at the beginning. Did you kill Hastings?"

His eyes flashed anger. He snarled, "None of us in here are guilty. Don't you know that?"

I held my temper. "Listen, Bobby. If you don't want

17

any help, you just say so, and I'll leave. I'm here as a favor to your cousin. He's a friend." I paused a moment.

He drew a deep breath and leaned back in his chair. Anger drained from his face as he shook his head, leaving a veneer of fear. "Hey, Man, don't pay no attention to me. It's just that—well, truth is, I'm scared." His Adam's apple bobbed nervously. "I'm scared like something you wouldn't believe. I'd always figured that if a guy was innocent, nothing could happen to him. But, I found out the hard way how wrong I was. Something bad can happen. When the system gets it in for you, something real bad can happen even if a guy don't deserve it."

I looked straight into his dark eyes. "I understand. Now, tell me your story."

Bobby eyed me warily for several moments, then released a long breath. "Not much to tell. I was framed." He hesitated, then hurried to add, "Look, I know a lot of cons claim that, but I *was*."

Suppressing my skepticism, I said, "Go on."

"Well, it was like this. Hastings learned that Lorene— that's his wife—that Lorene and me were having an affair. He didn't do nothing about it. Then several months later, he jumped me at the Double Eagle—that's a bar on the south side of Austin—but I beat him to the punch. Two days later, I was fired. I blew up. I grabbed my gun and threatened him. But I didn't kill him. I wanted to. Oh, how I wanted to." He paused, then added wryly, "But he wasn't worth the price I'd have to pay for killing him, so I left him in his office. I was standing in front of the elevator when I heard the shots."

"Then what?"

"I was scared. When the doors opened, I stepped into the elevator and left." He paused, studying me.

"Did anyone see you go into his office?"

"Some secretary. She saw me go in, but it wasn't his office. It was in the board room of his building."

"Building?"

"Yeah. Hastings' Real Estate. Ten stories. The board-room is on the top floor."

"What about when you left? She must have seen you leave the boardroom."

With a rueful grin, he shook his head, "Just my luck, she wasn't at her desk."

"Danny said something about a tape proving you didn't kill Hastings."

He nodded. "That's what I was told. About two weeks after I was arrested, some guy named Red went to my Uncle Liam and claimed he had a tape showing a Chink gunning down Hastings after I left the room. For ten thousand, we could have it. My uncle said the guy claimed the tape showed the killer's face."

"Where did this Red get the tape?"

"He said it came from the security camera. My uncle planned to get the money from the bank."

"And?"

"And the guy didn't show up where they were supposed to meet."

I frowned, "Your uncle—did he see the tape?"

"No."

Bobby displayed none of the giveaway traits of a liar. He looked me straight in the eye and didn't hesitate with his story. Either he was telling the truth, or he was an accomplished actor delivering well-rehearsed lines. I had a gut feeling he was telling the truth.

"So," he said, "what now?"

"So," I replied, "I have the transcript of the trial. I need to talk to the witnesses."

He laughed bitterly. "Won't do no good. I can tell you what they'll say."

I looked at him curiously, then nodded briefly. "I'm listening."

"First, there's the secretary. She'll say I went in the boardroom, and the next thing she knew, Hastings had been shot, and she saw me get on the elevator. Then there's Sam Bradford, the Lieutenant Governor, who swore I started the fight with Hastings at the Double Eagle."

"But you did hit him?"

He chuckled. "As hard as I could."

"Tell me about it."

With a sigh, he began, "I'd stopped in for a after-work drink at the Double Eagle. All of a sudden, Hastings and Bradford popped up. Before I knew what was happening, Hastings took a swing at me." With a shrug, he added, "He hit me on the shoulder and knocked me to the floor. Then he kicked me, but I got back up and swung at him. I didn't miss."

"Go on."

"And then there was my supervisor at A. A. Aggregates, L. D. Bryson, who testified that I told him I wanted to kill Hastings."

I frowned, "Did you?"

"Yeah, but I didn't mean it like that. I was mad. It was just a way to let off steam." He hesitated.

"Go on."

"What happened was Bryson fired me. He said I'd messed up on an important estimate that cost us thirteen thousand bucks. I didn't. Later, when I told Lorene, she said Hastings was behind it. He got me fired because I punched him out, not because Lorene was having an affair with me or because of a mistake at work. He had laughed about the affair."

"What happened then?"

"I went back and confronted Bryson. Naturally, he denied Hastings was involved, and that's when I lost it."

"That's when you said you'd kill Hastings?"

He nodded slowly.

"How long had you worked at A. A. Aggregates?"

"Ten years. It was my first job when I got out of high school."

I studied him several moments. I had asked all the questions I could think of. I forced a grin. "That's all I need for the time being, Bobby. I'd better get to work."

I started to hang up the receiver, but he stopped me. "Tony?"

"Yeah?"

He dragged the tip of his tongue across his dry lips. "What do you think?"

I studied him thoughtfully, feeling sorry for the guy. "I've got six days. A lot can happen in that time."

Bobby forced a weak smile. "I hope so."

After Bobby left, I spent a few minutes jotting down what I had learned on three-by-five cards, a timeworn method I'd used for years.

After slipping the cards into my pocket, I stared at the drab steel door that had closed behind Bobby. I hoped I was good enough to help him.

Chapter Four

Janice arched an eyebrow when I climbed back in the truck. "How did it go?"

I reached for my cell phone. "I think I believe him, but we've got a lot of legwork ahead of us."

"We don't have long. Do you think you can save him?"

"All we can do is try." I punched in Nathan Savage's number at Blevins' Investigations and had him find the name and address of the vendor who maintained the security video at Hastings Real Estate, ". . . and Nathan."

"Yeah."

"Call me back as soon as you have it. I won't be rolling into town for about three hours." I gave him my cell phone number and punched off.

During the drive back to Austin, Janice read the transcript aloud for me, pausing only to jot down the names of the four witnesses who provided what appeared to be irrefutable evidence.

The first was Sgt. Jack Carpenter, arresting officer. When he had searched Bobby Packard's apartment, he had discovered a Glock 21 handgun—a 9 mm, the same caliber as the slugs dug out of Hastings. I cringed. *What were the odds that another killer would use the same cal-iber handgun that Packard owned?*

Then there were the witnesses Packard had mentioned, Samuel Bradford, Lieutenant Governor-elect; Natalie Romero, Hastings' secretary; and finally L. D. Bryson, Bobby's supervisor at A. A. Aggregates and Asphalt.

"But, what can they tell you that isn't in the transcript?" Janice asked when I explained I wanted to talk to each of them in detail.

"They only answered the questions they were asked. After listening to the transcript, I can think of a few other questions."

"Like what?"

I flexed my fingers on the steering wheel, trying to arrange my thoughts. "Well, for example, we can't argue with the fact that Packard told his boss he wanted to kill Hastings. But on the other hand, Packard's supervisor said he was fired because he botched a major estimate, costing the company thirteen thousand dollars."

Janice studied me, puzzled. "So?"

"So. Look how long Packard had worked there. He was the estimate *supervisor*. It took him ten years to reach that position. There's no mention of previous mistakes. You're going to fire a valuable employee for one goof in ten years? And for only thirteen thousand dollars? That doesn't make sense. There had to be more behind it—an ulterior motive."

"Maybe he had made more mistakes."

I shrugged. "Maybe so. And maybe he was fired because Bradford insisted on it. That's what I mean. I just think there should have been more questions asked. Take the bartender, for example."

"What bartender?"

"The one working at the Double Eagle when Hastings and Packard fought. Why wasn't he questioned?

"Wouldn't that have been up to Packard's attorney?"

"Yeah. That's another part of this that puzzles me. Why didn't his attorney try to discredit some of the prosecution's assertions? For example, the transcript says nothing about matching the slugs to the Glock 21. Why not?"

At that moment, my cell phone rang. It was Savage with the name and address of Endicott Video. "Thanks, pal," I said. "Now, grab a pencil and paper. I have four witnesses I need addresses for."

Traffic on the highway from Huntsville to Austin was heavy, especially west of the city of Bryan, a corridor on Highway 21 usually filled bumper-to-bumper in both directions with students from Texas A & M heading to or returning from the nightlife in Austin.

I had just clicked off and handed the cell phone to Janice when a loud pop exploded under the pickup and the back end began gyrating wildly.

Janice screamed, "Tony!"

Blowout! I muttered a curse, firmly guiding the Silverado off the shoulder of the road to the grassy right-of-way and pumping the brakes lightly.

Without warning, a concrete drainage ditch four feet deep appeared in front of us.

I slammed on the brakes. "Hold on," I muttered between clenched teeth.

Janice didn't answer. I steeled myself for the impact.

We slid to a halt inches from the edge of the ditch.

For several seconds, neither of us spoke. I just sat staring straight ahead, my fists squeezing the steering wheel so hard my knuckles turned white.

After a few moments, her slender fingers still clutching the safety grip on the dash with a death grip, Janice whispered hoarsely, "That was close."

One thing about Janice was her knack for understatement. "Too close," I muttered.

We looked at each other. "Are you all right," I asked.

She nodded, "What happened?"

"Blowout," I muttered, climbing out and retrieving the jack from behind the seat.

Within minutes, I had changed the tire on the back left. Inspecting the blown tire, I noticed a tiny blemish on the sidewall. I touched my finger to it, and to my surprise, I found it was a small hole that appeared to be much more likely the result of a slug from a handgun than trash on the highway.

"What caused it?" Janice nodded to the ragged tire on the ground.

Shaking my head I replied, "There's no telling. Rock, glass, who knows? I need to pick up a spare tire first chance," I added, keeping my suspicions to myself, and remembering the phone call from the previous night. Was the tire truly just an accident, or was there some connection with the warning from the day before?

After a few minutes to steady our nerves and collect our thoughts, we pulled back on the highway. This time, I kept my eyes on the rearview and side mirrors.

"So now what?" Janice asked a few miles down the road.

Taking a deep breath, I said, "The video company. Red must have worked for the company to have had access to the security cameras."

She frowned at me. "What security cameras?"

I remembered she knew nothing of the alleged videotape. I quickly explained and concluded, "So if we're lucky, we might be able to run down the tape."

Her eyes widened in disbelief. "After all these years? How long has it been?"

With a sheepish grin, I replied, "Ten or eleven."

"And you really believe you can find the tape?"

I raised an eyebrow. "In all honesty?"

"Yes," she nodded vigorously, "in all honesty."

"No, I don't but I've got to try." A thought hit me. "Take a look at the transcript again. Is there any mention of a videotape?"

After fifteen minutes, she looked up. "Nothing," she said.

"Huh! That's odd."

Janice frowned at me. "What's odd?"

Keeping my eyes on the road both front and back, I replied, "If you were the district attorney and you have a video of Packard shooting Hastings, wouldn't you use it in court?"

"Certainly. What idiot wouldn't?"

"There are some, believe me. Anyway, if there was a video available, why wasn't it produced?"

Growing excited over a possible corroborative theory to support the existence of the tape, I answered my own question. "The tape wasn't used because the DA had no idea that it existed." I shot Janice a glance. "Most security cameras are hooked into a central location where images are recorded on a tape of some sort. I'll lay odds that in this case when the criminalists detailed the crime scene, they found no tape—or if they found a tape, someone had swapped it."

"Red!"

"Exactly."

Chapter Five

W ithin a few miles, we drove into the small village of Lincoln, where I pulled into a Wal-Mart to replace the blown tire. As the young technician changed the tire, he remarked at the puncture in the sidewall. "What did you hit here?"

"Beats me," I shook my head. "Piece of metal or something."

He poked a screwdriver in the depression. He grinned crookedly. "Sure someone wasn't shooting at you, mister?"

His question sent chills up my spine. I forced a laugh, "Positive."

Endicott Video was on South Congress beyond the Colorado River. I pulled into the parking lot on the north side of the white fieldstone building and glanced at Janice. "You want to come in?"

She smiled, dimpling her cheeks. "I should say so. I need to stretch my legs."

Inside a young woman smiled from behind a glass counter filled with video equipment. Similar counters

27

stood in front of the walls of either side. "Yes, sir. Can I help you?"

I glanced around. There were two doors behind the counters, both closed. "I hope so, Miss," I showed her my ID. "I'm a private investigator, and I'm looking for a man named Red who worked here ten or eleven years ago."

She frowned. "We don't have anyone that goes by Red. What's his last name?"

With a shrug, I replied, "I don't know." She raised a skeptical eyebrow. I explained, "I know it isn't much, but this Red guy might have some information that could save a man from execution at Huntsville next week."

She glanced at Janice and smiled apologetically, "I understand, but I don't know anyone by that name." Abruptly, she turned. "Just a minute. Let me see what I can find out." She opened one of the doors. She called out to a technician bent over a workbench in the adjoining room, "Hey, Kelly. You've been here longer than me. Did you ever know someone who worked for us by the name of Red?"

Keeping his eyes on his work, Kelly called back, "How long ago?"

"About ten years."

He shook his head, "That was before my time." He glanced around and, standing upright, shrugged. "Sorry, about the only one who would know for sure would be old Floyd. And he retired four or five years ago."

"This Floyd, does he have a last name?"

"Yeah. Holloman, Floyd Holloman. He used to live out east of Austin somewhere around the little town of Manor."

Floyd Holloman was easy to contact. Reaching his place at Box 2964, Star Route 7, Manor, Texas, was much more complicated. "Take Highway 290, and turn north on the second dirt road east of Wilson's Wrecking Yard," he explained over the telephone. "Then shoot a left on the dirt road before you reach the Barnes' place. The Barnes' place has a gate with steer horns on top. You've gone too far if you get there. About a mile down the road, there's a fork. Take the one to the right. My road is the second on the left after you go past a tin feeder barn."

I repeated each step, slowly enough so Janice could jot it all down.

As we wound our way along the twisted roads, Janice looked around at me. "Tony?"

"Yeah," I kept my eyes on the narrow dirt road.

"Is this what your job is really like? I mean, driving around and asking questions?"

I gave her a lopsided grin, "Pretty much."

She fell silent, staring thoughtfully out the window.

"Not much like Nick and Nora Charles in the movies, huh?"

"Well, to be honest, it isn't exactly what I thought."

I suppressed a grin. Like most of her impulses, this one appeared to be dying its own slow death. I tried to encourage it along its journey by adding, "Most of the time, the job is pretty dull. It's legwork, questions, digging for information . . . pretty dull."

With a disappointed shrug, she grinned weakly, "I just thought it would be more exciting."

I chuckled, "It's like what a pilot once told me about flying. 'Flying,' he said, 'is hours and hours of absolute boredom, punctuated by moments of sheer terror.'"

She laughed.

What neither of us knew was that Floyd Holloman would put us on a road laden with moments of sheer terror.

Chapter Six

The driveway to Floyd Holloman's circled a pond the size of a football field and ended in a graveled parking lot in front of a double-wide manufactured home sitting in the shade of a broad canopy of ancient pecan and oak.

A roly-poly gentleman in bib overalls and a blue cotton shirt, with a straw hat perched on his head, stood in the middle of a pumpkin patch, staring at us curiously. He reminded me of the Pillsbury Doughboy in farmer's garb.

Even before we stopped, he was walking toward us, his hand held over his head as a gesture of greeting. "Howdy," he called out as we climbed out of the pickup.

I nodded, "Mr. Holloman?"

He stopped in front of us, an amiable smile on his full face. "Yes, sir. Floyd Holloman." He spoke with a nasal twang.

"I'm Tony Boudreaux and this is Janice Coffman-Morrison," I said, extending my hand. "I talked to you earlier."

Despite his advanced age, his grip was firm. "Pleased to know you folks. What can I do for you?"

"You retired a few years back from Endicott Video."

A slight frown wrinkled is forehead. "Six years ago I started drawing my Social Security."

"When you worked at Endicott Video, did you happen to know a man named Red?"

The frown on his face faded into shocked disbelief. "Red? Red Tompkins? You mean he finally turned up?"

A surge of excitement raced through my veins. "So you knew him?"

He nodded emphatically, "I should say so. We worked together four or five years before he just up and disappeared. Went into a Chinese funeral home and never came out. Where is that worthless hound anyway?"

I shook my head. "That's what I'm trying to find out."

"You mean—I'm sorry. I just assume . . ." he shifted his gaze to Janice, then back to me. "He still hasn't shown up, huh?"

"No."

"And you're looking for him."

"Yes."

He studied me for several seconds. "Why now? He's been gone ten or eleven years."

"There's a man on death row in Huntsville scheduled for execution next week. The story I heard was that Red had some video film that would prove the guy's innocence, but he disappeared."

Holloman digested my explanation, and then suddenly his face lit in understanding. "Video film, huh? So that's what that rascal was talking about. I never could figure it out."

Janice and I exchanged surprised looks. "What do you mean that was what he was talking about?"

He removed his hat and dragged his arm across his forehead. "Well, sir, I'll never forget. It was October 3. We finished up our daily itinerary early that day, and Red had me detour over to the west side of Austin to a Chinese funeral home." He hesitated, his face knotted in concentration. "I can't remember the name, but it was on Balcones Drive. Red had been acting kind of funny for the last couple days. When I asked what was at the funeral home, he grinned and told me I'd know soon enough."

"And that was it?"

"Yep. Well, except he did something funny."

"Like what?"

"Well, sir, just before he climbed out of the truck to go inside the funeral home, he patted the heel of his cowboy boot. He always wore cowboy boots—thought of hisself as a cowboy. You know . . . jeans, flowery shirts, big belt buckles."

I frowned, puzzled. "What was so funny about patting the heel of his boot?"

"It wasn't that. It was what he said."

Impatiently, I prompted him. "Which was . . ."

"I never understood what he meant."

"And?"

"He was funny that way, Red was."

I was growing exasperated, having to drag information from him piece by piece. "I understand. So, what did he say?"

He raised an eyebrow. "He patted his boot heel and said that was what was going to make him rich."

Janice looked up at me with a puzzled look on her face. I shook my head. "Rich? I don't understand, Mr. Holloman. What did he mean by that?"

The elderly man shrugged. "The boot heel. It was hollow. Red carried a spare twenty in the heel of his boot so he'd never be broke." He wagged his finger at us. "I'll wager that if he was figuring on selling film valuable enough to make him rich, he's bound to have carried it in the heel of his boot." He paused, looking up at me with smug satisfaction. "Do you understand now?"

I understood, but I wasn't quite sure if I truly believed Floyd Holloman. "He had hollowed out the heel? Is that what you're telling us?"

Holloman nodded.

"How . . . did it work? Did the heel come off or what?" I couldn't visualize it.

"Nope. The bottom of the heel just turned to the side. He showed me once when we ran out of money at a bar. He just pulled the boot off, twisted the heel, and pulled out his twenty."

"And you say, he never came back out of the Chinese funeral home."

He glanced toward his trailer house. "You folks care for some sweet tea? I worked up a thirst out in the pumpkin patch."

Janice peered at the baking sun, shading her eyes with her hand. "I wouldn't mind at all, Mr. Holloman."

Leading the way to the small brick patio in front of the house, Floyd Holloman continued his story. "I waited outside the funeral home for about thirty minutes, getting more and more ticked off at Red. Finally, I went inside. There were two or three funerals going on. Red wasn't nowhere to be found. I run down one of those Asian guys who worked there, and he said a red-headed man had come in earlier and walked straight out the back door."

Holloman gestured to some lawn chairs in the shade. "Sit. I'll get the tea." He tossed his straw hat on the round, glass-topped patio table.

While he was inside, Janice whispered, "Do you think he's telling the truth?"

"He has to be. The story's too cockeyed to make up."

She shook her head. "It is that."

He returned carrying a tray with a pitcher of tea, three ice-filled glasses, and a bowl of sugar. "Help yourself.

Sweeten to taste," he said with a grin, setting the tray on the table.

"So, like I said," he continued, plopping down in a lawn chair, "Red walked out the back door. I went out to see if I could find him. All I found was an alleyway. But there was no sign of him." He paused. "Then I went back to the truck. I waited until all the funerals were over and the place was empty except for the owners." He shook his head, "Red never showed up. And as far as I know, he hasn't until this day." He sipped his tea. "Cops came around later and asked a few questions. That was it."

I pondered his account of the incident. One thing puzzled me. "You said it was October 3. How can you be so certain after all these years?"

He laughed, "Are you married, son?"

I glanced at Janice. A light blush colored her cheeks. "I used to be, but not now."

"Well, if you was, then you know how wives can get if you forget a birthday. My Ruby's birthday, rest her soul, was October 4. I completely forgot about it puzzling over what on earth had come of Red." He shook his head. "She sure gave me blazes." He grinned at Janice and me. "That, young lady and young man, is why I remember the date so clear."

We laughed along with him. Despite being near the end of October, the day was hot, and the cool shade was a pleasant relief. I looked around. "Have you lived out here long?"

He grew somber. "Five years or so. Ruby and me bought it so we could retire. We'd been together forty-one years." His forehead wrinkled and his brows knit in grief. "We always figured we could hit fifty, maybe even sixty years together. She passed away our first year here, sudden-like. We never had the chance to enjoy our retirement."

I regretted having asked the question. I glanced at

Janice, then rose to my feet. "Thank you, Mr. Holloman. You've been more than helpful."

In the pickup, I jotted my notes on the ubiquitous three-by-five cards. When Janice asked about them, I explained, "They help me keep things straight. Sometimes when I rearrange the cards, I see the issue from a different perspective."

When I finished, I slipped them in my pocket and turned the ignition key. The engine roared to life.

Chapter Seven

We rode in silence for several moments. "I feel sorry for him," Janice whispered.

"Yeah," I replied, wondering how I could handle losing Janice after forty years. I pushed the thought from my head, returning to our present conundrum. I couldn't help wondering if the assertion that an Asian shot Hastings and the fact that Red Tompkins disappeared in a Chinese funeral home was more than coincidence.

I bounced the idea off Janice.

She looked up at me hopefully. "Do you think there's a connection?"

"Think about it. Red goes to Bobby's uncle and claims he had a film showing the real killer was an Asian. For ten thousand, Bobby can have the film." I hesitated as my brain pulled off a *Sherlock Holmes*. "Obviously, since Red had something valuable, he wanted to get the best price. And what better way than to play two involved parties against each other?"

"You mean, he was trying to sell it to some Chinaman at the funeral home?" Her voice reflected her surprise.

"Why not? He asked ten thousand from Packard.

Maybe he thought he could raise the ante at the funeral home." I paused for a moment, trying to sort the myriad thoughts tumbling through my head.

Janice gave me the next little nudge. "But how would he have known to go to the funeral home?"

I studied the highway ahead for several moments before answering. "It stands to reason, if you want to sell someone a tape of a murder, you'll go to the one most likely to be hurt by the tape, right?"

She nodded, her eyes lighting up in understanding. "I follow you. In other words, Red Tompkins must have recognized the Asian on the tape and knew that either he or someone who knew him was at the funeral home."

I winked at her, "Yeah, yeah, I think you might have something there."

A big smile played over her face, dimpling her cheeks. "Now what?"

Glancing at my watch, I replied, "It's just after four. Let's go see Danny and bring him up to date."

She caught her breath. Her eyes narrowed. "Danny? O'Banion? The mob boss?"

I chuckled, "Alleged mob underboss."

"Why him?"

"I didn't tell you?"

"Tell me what?"

"Robert Packard, the guy on death row is Danny O'Banion's cousin. Danny O'Banion is a legitimate client of Blevins' Investigations."

Janice frowned at me in disbelief.

I gave her a gentle smile. "Don't worry. He won't bite."

Her frown deepened, "I don't know if I want to meet him."

I teased her. "Why? Afraid of your reputation?"

Fire shot from her eyes. "Of course not. It's just that he's a criminal."

"Maybe, but a charming criminal. You'll see. Like I said, he won't bite."

"He'd better not. I'll bite back. But, I can tell you now, I won't like him," she snapped, her clipped words sounded like the staccato of a machine gun.

I arched an eyebrow. "At least be gracious."

She sniffed that inimitable, patented little-rich-girl sniff. "Oh, I'll be gracious. Don't worry about that. I've had plenty of lessons on being gracious, and I'll probably need every single one of them tonight."

All I could do was roll my eyes.

Danny agreed to a 5:30 meeting at the County Line Barbecue on Bee Tree Road. It was a rustic establishment that served the most mouth-watering, juicy barbecue in all of the South, with the exception of that cooked by my uncle Patric Thibodeaux in his famed converted freezer chest over in Louisiana.

On the way to County Line Barbecue, I stopped by a telephone booth and thumbed through the yellow pages. There, on Balcones Drive I found the Chinese funeral home of which Hollomon had spoken, the Kwockwing Funeral Home.

When we turned into the County Line Parking Lot sometime later, I spotted Danny's black Lincoln Towncar at the back of the lot. Gargantuan Huey stepped from the Lincoln and opened the rear door as we climbed from the Silverado.

Janice gasped when she saw Huey. "Tony," she whispered, her voice strangled.

Chuckling, I whispered, "That's Godzilla. His favorite hobby is pulling legs and arms off people Danny doesn't like."

She looked around sharply, her eyes scolding me. "I'm not that dumb," she muttered.

Danny greeted us with his trademark grin, a roguish smile that made you think you were the only one in his presence. "Tony, boy, good to see you."

We shook, and I introduced him to Janice. Charm oozed from his pores as he turned on his Irish magic. "You said she was pretty, Tony, but you didn't tell me she's an angel."

I lifted an eyebrow. I'd never mentioned a word to him about Janice, but I grinned at that old Irish blarney. And naturally Janice blushed, and naturally Danny kept it up. He took her elbow and guided her into the restaurant and, obviously ignored by the two, Huey and I brought up the rear, a portent of the evening to come.

Danny was in rare form.

Occasionally dropping me a tidbit of the conversation, he monopolized Janice until the platters of barbecue arrived.

Janice frowned when she noticed Huey did not have a plate in front of him. "Huey's a vegetarian," Danny explained with a jocular lilt in his words. "And he never eats dinner. It causes him to gain weight. Isn't that right, Huey?"

Janice looked around at me, as if asking whether she should believe Danny or not. I simply shrugged.

And Huey simply grunted. "Yeah, Boss," he answered, which, while it paled next to Hamlet's, was for him an effusive soliloquy.

The juicy barbecue was served with ice-cold beer in frosty mugs. A couple years earlier, I had joined Alcoholics Anonymous. Since then, I might have tottered once or twice from the wagon, but mostly, I had kept the pledge.

While Danny put the barbecue away and washed it down with gulps of cold beer, I sipped at my mug and brought him up to date. "When you suggested an Asian triad might be behind the murder, I was skeptical, Danny. But now, along with the allegation that the gunman was Asian and Tompkins disappearing in that Chinese funeral home, I'm beginning to think along the same lines. Can you and your connections give me any help with the triads around here, in Austin?"

Danny hesitated. He dabbed at his lips with his napkin. The blithe tone in his voice grew serious. "Look, Tony. My people deal with the triads. If I start nosing around, I'm begging for an unmarked grave under an expressway. Understand?"

Clearly puzzled, Janice glanced back and forth from Danny to me, but she remained silent.

Drawing a deep breath, I released it slowly. "I understand."

He cut his eyes to Huey, then Janice, sending me a message. Reverting to his blithe chatter, he said. "I knew you would, buddy." Then he turned his attention back to Janice. "You look like the kind of person who would enjoy the gambling tables in Monte Carlo," he purred.

"Oh, I've been there," she exclaimed. "Have you?"

"What a small world," he remarked, focusing his full attention on her. "I was there just two months ago, on vacation." I kept quiet. Danny's vacations were all mob-oriented.

"Me too," she gushed, "but it was last summer."

"Which was your favorite casino?"

She clapped her hands. "The Casino de Monte Carlo. I loved the Bohemian glass chandeliers and the rococo ceilings."

"The belle epoque architecture impressed me most," Danny replied. "And in an aesthetic sense, I especially appreciated the twenty-eight Ionic columns running across the Renaissance Hall to the main gambling hall."

I wanted to gag. *Danny wouldn't know an Ionic column if one sat down at a poker table with him*, I told myself.

For the next few minutes, they reminisced over the glamour and intrigue of the little principality, of restaurants such as the Café de Paris, and hotels like Loew's Monte Carlo. She fawned over his every word, and the truth was, I was growing jealous.

During a lull in the *ooh's* and *aah's* of their experiences in Monte Carlo, Janice excused herself to the powder room. As soon as she left the table, Danny turned to Huey. "Get the Lincoln, Huey. Time to go. I'll be right out. I want to tell Miss Coffman-Morrison good night."

You bet, you jerk, I thought to myself. *You just want her to fawn over you once more.*

When Huey closed the door behind him, Danny turned abruptly to me. "Lei Sun Huang heads up the Ying On triad in Austin. There's a tong also, the Sing Leon. Joey Soong runs it."

His sudden burst of information caught me unexpectedly, but I managed to ask, "Do you know anything about them?"

Danny's eyes narrowed as he rose quickly to his feet and whispered harshly, "No one knows anything about Lei Sun. He's the original mystery man. Joey Soong is all right. The Asians around here are just like everyone else—some good, some bad. In fact, most of the second-generation Asians are just as much corn-fed Texans as you are a crawfish-eating Cajun."

He glanced over his shoulder. "Now, listen to me. I told you nothing, you hear? Figure out some way to explain how you came up with those names if someone should ask, but don't involve me."

My resentment toward him melted into gratitude. He had stuck out his neck for me big-time. "Thanks, Danny. I—"

He cut me off with that cockeyed grin of his spreading across his freckled face. "And tell the little lady she's quite a stunner. If she gets tired of you, she can look me up."

"Get out of here," I growled with a grin.

Janice was disappointed when she returned and found Danny had departed.

"He had to run," I said, sarcasm dripping from my words. "He had a guy to rub out."

She just glared at me.

Chapter Eight

Clouds had moved in, obscuring the starlight. As always, traffic was heavy on Bee Tree Road, but I managed to sneak into a slot in the middle of a line of raging lunatics heading for the Daytona raceway called Loop 360.

The oncoming headlights lit up the interior of the pickup like strobes, with flashes of brilliant light.

I glanced sidelong at Janice. "Well, what did you think about Danny O'Banion?"

"Despite everything I've heard about him, he is charming—handsome too. And he's traveled."

Jealously flashed its green eyes when I heard the trace of awe in her voice. I wanted to say he wasn't that handsome or charming, but I held my tongue.

"The people he works for must think he is very smart, very intelligent to have the position he has. He has to be a very important person to them, don't you think?"

I don't know if I sensed a condescending nuance in her last remark or if it was my imagination.

"Well, don't you?"

What could I say? I had no idea our dinner would result in her obvious infatuation with Danny. How could I say disparaging things about him when I was the one who had jokingly called him charming. *Me and my big mouth.*

"Well?" she looked around at me, puzzled. "Don't you think he's an important person in his organization?"

I shot her a glance. "Do you know what kind of organization you're talking about?"

"Certainly. But still, isn't he important even in that kind of organization?"

With a defeated shrug, I nodded. "Yeah," I said with no enthusiasm and even less conviction, "he's important."

Janice stared at me a moment, obviously surprised at my indifference. "Tony? Are you jealous of Danny?"

"What?" I feigned shock. "Me? Jealous of Danny O'Banion? Not on your life."

She peered closer into my face. A triumphant smirk played over her face. "You are," she exclaimed, "you are! You're jealous of him."

I almost squeezed the steering wheel in two when I replied, "No way. If you want to believe the nonsense he was handing you, that's your problem. But one thing is certain, I am not jealous of Danny O'Banion."

She sat back and crossed her arms. I glanced at her, and in the glow of oncoming headlights, I could make out a smug grin on her face.

I was seething, but I knew that sooner or later the hand on the clock would get back to twelve. In other words, eventually everyone gets what he deserves. What surprised me this time was how quickly the hand reached twelve.

My cell phone rang. I answered. Instantly, my anger fled. I glanced out of the corner of my eyes at Janice. I deliberately kept my voice very casual. "Yeah, I'm fine. Sure, no problem. Tomorrow will be great. You know how to find me? Good. See you then."

"Who was that?" Janice asked when I punched off.

I shrugged, "No one important."

She persisted, "Who?"

"You don't know her."

Her curiosity egged her on. "Tell me anyway. Is it some kind of secret?"

"No," I looked around at her innocently, "it isn't a secret. It's someone I knew back in Louisiana who's coming to town tomorrow and wants to bunk on my couch for a couple nights."

"An old boyhood chum?" Frustration was evident in her voice.

I shook my head and suppressed a smug grin of my own. Casually, I replied, "No. My ex-wife."

Chapter Nine

Janice coughed and sputtered, "Your what?"

Innocently, I replied, "My ex-wife, Diane. I've told you about her."

"Yes, but—but—"

Donning the most naïve, innocuous expression I could manage, I looked at her. "But what?"

She gaped at me. "What's she doing here?"

"The National Park Service transferred her to Johnson City, you know, LBJ's boyhood home. She needs a place to flop until she finds a place of her own."

"But . . . why you?" she was sputtering now.

"She doesn't know anyone around here," I paused, glancing at her. "Why? What's the matter?" I asked with an ingenuous air. "You're not jealous, are you?"

I've got to give Janice credit. She was much more candid than me on the jealously issue. "Yes, I'm jealous," she spat out. "And I don't mind saying so. I don't want that—that—"

Now it was my time to chuckle. "Easy. Remember, you're a lady."

She glared at me. "Oh, you . . . just shut up," she muttered and jerked around in the seat folding her arms across her chest. She did not speak to me the remainder of the drive home, nor did she bother to say good night. She just jumped out of the truck and slammed the door.

Because she had taken such delight in my being jealous, I wasn't about to tell Janice that there was no way on this green earth that I planned to let Diane stay with me. By the time she arrived in Austin the next afternoon, I would have a temporary spot for her, and I knew exactly who could take care of it for me.

As soon as I closed my apartment door behind me, I called Jack Edney, an old friend with whom I had taught high school years earlier. The lucky stiff was now living a life of luxury, having inherited about six million dollars before taxes. He had invested a portion of the inheritance in an apartment complex out on Ben White Road near Highway 290 that led directly to Johnson City.

Jack owed me. Not only had I been instrumental in his inheriting the six million instead of only one or two, but he was also guilty of murdering several of my exotic fish and causing brain damage in the sole survivor when he had drunkenly urinated in my aquarium. Oscar, the albino tiger barb that looked like a copper penny, had swum only in circles since Jack's assault.

It's amazing what you can wrangle from people who owe you. Within five minutes I had arranged a nice apartment for Diane. Naturally, I neglected to tell Jack that back in Vicksburg she had once had an affair with his older brother, W. R. She could surprise him with that little tidbit later if she so chose.

As I replaced the receiver in the cradle I hesitated, remembering Danny's information regarding the local triads and tongs. On impulse, I called Joe Ray Burrus, my only dependable source with Austin P. D. He was off, so I called him at home.

"Hey, Tony. What's going on?"

"Tell me something, Joe Ray," I said, getting straight to the point. "What do you know about the Asian triads and tongs in Austin?"

He uttered a low curse. "Not much except they hate each other."

"How's that?"

"Well, it's kinda hard to say. They're sort of like social or business clubs—you know, like the Knights of Columbus or Masons or clubs like that. They have their beliefs, and their own way of doing things. I don't understand them. I don't think any white guy understands them."

"So? Every culture has its own practices."

"Yeah, maybe so. But here in Austin, the tongs and triads can't stand each other."

"Why's that?"

"Triads, like the one we got here, the Ying On triad, is allegedly involved in criminal activities. An old Chink geezer, Lei Sun Huang, is the head honcho. But the tong is like a fraternal organization. Really, it's more like the Knights of Columbus or Lions Club than a triad."

"Fraternal? Bingo and that sort of thing?"

Joe Ray snorted, "I don't know about bingo, but from what I hear, it's how they do business. Most of the tongs are good old boys, like us. As I understand it, the Sing Leon tong is like our Chamber of Commerce. There are certain ways to practice business and it's done through the tong."

"So, the tongs aren't criminal."

"Not usually."

I rolled my eyes. "That's what I like about you, Joe

Ray. You know exactly what you're talking about all the time."

He chuckled, "Hey, pal no one knows what those Chinese guys are doing, or what they're talking about *any* of the time."

The phone rang early next morning, just after 6:00. It was Janice and her voice was snippy. "You don't have to let that woman stay with you. I have found her an apartment," she emphasized *that woman,* making the words sound sleazy.

I wanted to laugh, but knew better. I played it seriously. "Why, Janice. That's very decent of you." I contemplated whether I should tell her arrangements had already been made or just let her stew.

Wisdom dictated that I should tell her because if I didn't, she'd be angry all over again when she found out.

"But, the truth is, I wasn't about to let Diane stay with me. I called Jack last night, and he arranged an apartment for her in his complex west of town, but I do appreciate your thinking of her."

Her reply surprised me for up until this incident she had never been so forthright about her feelings. "I wasn't thinking of that woman. I was thinking of me."

For a moment, I was speechless but, finally the words I was struggling for rolled off my lips. "I was thinking of you too."

From there the conversation grew mushy, even maudlin. Finally, I asked her if she wanted to go with me that day. "More legwork?"

"I'm afraid so. I've got to interview Lorene Hasting, the widow, and the other witnesses. Pretty boring stuff."

She hesitated. "Give me a rain check. I have to get ready for the Halloween party tonight. You're still going, aren't you?"

"What do you think? I have my devil's costume all ready."

She giggled. "You're going to be the devil tonight, huh?"

"In more ways than one."

She giggled again. "Pick me up at nine."

"See you then."

She blew me a kiss over the phone. I couldn't believe it when I returned it. What was that woman doing to me? But whatever it was, I had to admit I wasn't doing much to stop her.

Chapter Ten

I shivered when I stepped outside a few minutes later. A small front had moved through during the night, and the thermometer on the porch put the temperature in the forties.

Popping back inside, I grabbed a nylon windbreaker and straightened my tie in the mirror. Just as I rushed out the door, the phone rang. "Now what?" I muttered.

It was Jack Edney. "Tony? Hope I didn't wake you."

"I was just leaving," I replied impatiently. "Can I call you back this evening? I've got a long drive ahead of me."

His voice grew animated. "Hey, I'll ride along. I can tell you what I've been thinking about."

I came up with a fast lie. "Sorry, Jack. Janice is going with me."

He chuckled lecherously. "Never mind. I'd just be in the way."

"I'll call when I get back."

"Okay, but I've got to tell you about it. You can be thinking it over."

Annoyed by his persistence, but remembering the favor he had done me by finding an apartment for Diane, I agreed. "What?"

"Now that I have all this money, I want to do some good. I want to run for city council in the primary next March. I want to make Austin a safer place to raise children. I want you to be my campaign manager."

"What?" I was stunned.

Hastily he added, "Don't say no right away. Think it over. I'll talk to you tonight." He hung up before I had a chance to refuse.

Shaking my head, I zipped the windbreaker. *Jack and his millions. What will he come up with next?*

Lorene Hastings was a forty-year-old woman who could have passed for twenty-seven or -eight. I could see how Bobby Packard had been attracted to her. Her wide-set green eyes provided a striking contrast to the shiny auburn hair that lay about her shoulders.

I had called earlier, and she was expecting me.

Her condo overlooked Lake Travis. The view from the glassed-in living room was spectacular. Farther than the eye could see, sixty-three miles of blue water sparkled amid the emerald hills lining the lake, at some places four and a half miles wide.

Gesturing to a Victorian wingback chair trimmed with rosewood, Lorene Hastings perched on the edge of the sofa. A silver coffee service sat on the table between us. She opened a diamond-encrusted cigarette case and offered me a Virginia Slim. I declined, having given up coffin nails ten years earlier.

She lit one and inhaled. She released the smoke slowly, squinting her green eyes against the thin tendrils curling upward, almost as if steeling herself for the interview. "So, you're here about Bobby?"

I leaned forward, resting my elbows on my knees. I had no time to waste. There were only four days left after today. "Do you think Robert Packard killed your husband?"

Her eyes lost their focus as she pondered the question. When they came back into focus, she turned them on me. "No. Oh, I know the evidence supported the prosecution, but Bobby was a gentle, caring man. That's why I loved him. He couldn't have killed Albert. He was not the kind to look for trouble."

"How did you meet?"

For the next few minutes, she retraced the history of their relationship. "You see," she added, "my husband Albert and I remained together for the sake of his career. It was a marriage in name only. We had separate bedrooms, separate lives. He had no problem with my finding other—" she shrugged, completely indifferent to my reactions, "you know, companions."

I nodded.

She continued. "I'd had other . . . ah . . . friends before. They never bothered him. To be honest, none of this would have happened if Albert hadn't taken a swing at Bobby that night at the Double Eagle."

"You think it was because he was governor-elect and afraid of the publicity?"

She raised an eyebrow. "If he wanted to stop our affair, he could have. He knew Bobby and I were seeing each other. We'd been together for almost a year—throughout the entire campaign—although we kept it quiet." She shook her head and chuckled ruefully. "And we did keep it quiet. You know the straight-to-the-jugular mindset of the media today. They would have ripped Albert apart."

"Maybe he was thinking ahead to the years he would be in office when he jumped Bobby."

She laughed, not quite a sneer, but close to it. "You don't know much about politics, do you, Mr. Boudreaux?"

"No, Ma'am, I don't."

"With very few exceptions, once you're in office, you're there to stay. Criticism, scandal, shame—they all

roll off your back. Look at our state and national politics."
She took another deep drag on her cigarette and shook her
head.

"So why did your husband go after Bobby in the bar?"

She shrugged. "Albert was drunk. No other reason."

"Is that why he had Bobby fired? The fight?"

Her eyes twinkled. "Albert had a tremendous ego. He
could never forget the whipping Bobby gave him." She
shook her head. "Nobody, but nobody got the best of
Albert Hastings. He got even one way or another."

"Let me ask you this, Mrs. Hastings. Who benefitted
from your husband's death? In other words, if it wasn't a
murder of passion, who stood to gain the most?"

She studied me. "Do you believe Bobby is innocent?"

I pondered her question. "That isn't for me to say, but
the truth is, there are a few unanswered questions bothering me, questions that make me wonder if he did murder
your husband."

Lorene Hastings arched an eyebrow. "I see. So, in
answer to your question, I benefited because of insurance,
prestige, and that sort of thing. Sam Bradford benefited
because he took over the governor's job which led to his
election as a U.S. Senator, and Don Landreth, Albert's
campaign manager, went on to become President Bonner's
campaign manager in the last two national elections."

"Landreth?" I frowned. "I haven't heard of him. He
didn't testify at the trial."

She shrugged. "He was Albert's campaign manager for
years, but to answer your question, I didn't kill Albert.
Don had no motive because he had no way of knowing
Charlie Bonner would pick him to run his presidential
campaign." She paused, took a deep drag off her cigarette
and blew the smoke out sharply. "So that leaves Sam
Bradford."

"Any ideas why Bradford would do something like that?"

She shook her head. "Politicians are scum, Mr. Boudreaux. To attain their goals, they'll stoop to whatever level necessary—lies, theft, even murder. Campaign managers aren't much better." Her brows knitting in a frown, she added, "But something more was going on. I don't know what but two days after Albert's death, his office was ransacked. Someone wanted something Albert had."

"What does Bradford want out of all of this?"

She looked at me as if she were staring at the world's biggest idiot. "Why, to be president, of course."

Of course. I should have known. How stupid of me. I rose and extended my hand. "Thanks for your time, Mrs. Hastings."

"Have I helped Bobby?"

"Well, you've given me something to chew on," I said, trying gracefully to skirt her question.

"I hope so," she said sadly. "I still love him."

Back in my truck, I committed the interview to my note cards. As I jotted down the information, I remembered a remark Bobby Packard had made. I shuffled back through my cards until I found it. "He wasn't worth the price I'd have to pay for killing him, so I left."

Lorene Hastings' assessment of Bobby Packard supported his statement. "A gentle caring man. He was not the kind to look for trouble."

Well, looking or not, I told myself. He's sure found himself neck-deep in it.

Chapter Eleven

Sgt. Jack Carpenter was the arresting officer. He had testified that when he searched Bobby Packard's apartment, he had discovered a Glock handgun, purportedly the same caliber slugs the M. E. dug out of Hastings.

My first call was to Chief Ramon Pachuca, with whom I had developed an amiable relationship over the last few years. He appreciated the fact I deferred to Austin P. D., always asking permission before intruding into their sphere of authority. I told him I wanted to talk to Carpenter if he didn't mind. He didn't. "How soon can you get over here?" he asked.

"Fifteen minutes."

"He'll be waiting." I beamed at my luck. Who says politeness doesn't pay?

Carpenter was a tall, gray-haired plainclothes cop with narrow shoulders and wide hips—a perfect example of the pear-shaped man. From the expression on his face, I could tell he was ticked off having to talk to me.

"Only one or two questions, Sergeant. They'll take no more than a couple minutes."

Chapter Twelve

My next stop was Natalie Romero, Hastings' secretary at the time of the murder. According to the receptionist at Hastings' Real Estate, Romero had resigned a few years earlier when she married the Reverend John Simms, the new minister of her church.

I knew I was living right when I learned the current receptionist also attended the same church.

Natalie Romero Simms answered on the first ring. At first she seemed reluctant to grant me an interview, but I assured her there would be no publicity, negative or otherwise, of this investigation. "It is for an individual client, not the police. And a man's life is at stake," I added, experiencing a tinge of guilt in deliberately appealing to her Christian compassion.

She consented, and fifteen minutes later I knocked on her door.

As soon as she answered the door, I knew her husband was a charismatic minister. She wore no makeup, and her hair was pulled into a severe bun. She wore a high-necked, long-sleeved blouse, and her black skirt dragged on the floor.

She invited me into her living room and offered tea. With an open smile, I declined. "I know you're busy, Mrs. Simms, so I'll be brief. I read the transcript of the trial. You testified that Robert Packard entered the board room without an appointment."

She nodded.

"Then what?"

Her eyes glazed over for a moment as her thoughts drifted back ten years. She stared at the flowers on her wallpaper as she recounted that day. "I hurried into the boardroom after the man, but Mr. Hastings told me everything was all right. He could handle the situation, so I went back out to my desk." She paused. Her cheeks colored slightly. "Then, I went into the ladies' room. I was drying my hands when I heard three shots. Of course, I didn't know that's what they were then. I hurried out into the hall. When I did, I saw Robert Packard step into the elevator." She paused once again.

"Go on, Mrs. Simms. You're doing fine."

Her lips quivered. She chewed on the bottom one as she collected her emotions. "I hurried into the boardroom. Mr. Hastings was lying on the floor, the front of his shirt red with blood."

"Did you see anyone else around?"

"You mean, after I heard the shots?"

I hesitated. "Before or after."

"Well, when I headed into the powder room, an Asian gentleman was stepping off the elevator. And then afterward, all I saw were those coming into the hall wondering what the commotion was."

An Asian! Trying to keep the excitement from my voice, I asked. "What about the boardroom? Did you see anyone in there?"

"Besides Mr. Hastings, no."

"What about the Asian gentleman. Did you see him?"

"No."

Nodding slowly, I replied. "I want you to think back, Mrs. Simms, to the boardroom. Other than the door to the reception room, how many doors does it have?"

Her forehead wrinkled in concentration. "Let me think. It's been a long time, you know."

I nodded.

"There was one going to the executive lounge and—let me think—one, two, three. No—no, I'm wrong. There are only two. One opens into a large storeroom and the other to the executive lounge. That's right, there are two doors in the boardroom not counting the main door—I'm certain," she added with a smile of satisfaction on her face.

"Did you ever go into the storeroom?"

"Oh, yes. Regularly."

"Did it have an exit other than into the boardroom?"

She shook her head.

I grinned sheepishly. "I don't suppose you ever went into the executive lounge."

She blushed violently. "Oh, heavens no. I—"

"Sorry, Mrs. Simms, but I had to ask."

She smiled demurely. "That's all right, Mr. Boudreaux."

"One other question. There was a video camera in the office, but there was no mention of it in the trial transcript. It seems to me that would have offered irrefutable proof of the murderer."

"It most certainly would have, but one of the technicians had installed the tape incorrectly. It didn't expose, or whatever it does."

Stifling my excitement at her last remark, I rose and offered my hand. "I see. Thank you very much for your time."

"You're more than welcome, Mr. Boudreaux."

I hesitated. "If you don't mind, Mrs. Simms, I just thought of one more question about the technician who serviced the videotapes. By any chance do you happen to remember what he looked like?"

Her eyes brightened. "Oh, dear me yes. A sweet, fair complected young man with red hair. He always stopped and chatted with me when he changed tapes or whatever it was he did. Red—ah, his name's Red—"

I supplied the name for her, "Tompkins?"

"That's it!" she exclaimed. "Red Tompkins."

Another piece of the puzzle fell into place.

Back in my pickup, I pulled out my cards. I glanced up and spotted the edge of the drapes in Mrs. Simms' picture window pulled aside a few inches. She was watching. I smiled, waved, and then quickly jotted my notes.

I mused over the information I had garnered from Mrs. Simms. There was no question that she was telling the truth, and that her testimony had been damning. Packard barged in; she heard shots; she saw Packard hurrying into the elevator.

But, if the alleged film was to be believed, someone else had been present. And she had seen the Asian emerging from the elevator. I discounted his hiding in the storeroom after doing Hastings. Chances are the police would have searched it as part of the crime scene. But there a distinct possibility the killer could have darted into the executive lounge and escaped through a window—if there was a window.

I glanced at my watch as I made a note to check that possibility. 10:00. Plenty of time to run down Sen. Sam Bradford and Don Landreth, Hastings' campaign manager.

Bradford was in Washington, which effectively squelched any interview with him, so I concentrated on

Landreth, whom I managed to run down at his ranch out-side Marble Falls, fifty or so miles to the west.

Placing a call, I got Landreth's voice mail. I left my name, number, and a brief explanation of the purpose of my call. I considered driving over, but if he was not around I'd have wasted two or three hours that could not be spared.

My stomach growled, and I realized I had not eaten since early morning. I glanced around, searching for someplace to silence the gurgling sounds coming from my belly.

I stopped at the first light. A maroon car pulled up behind me. Years and makes are beginning to elude me. At my age, I can discern a car and a pickup, but that's about the extent of my expertise.

I drove through McDonald's for fries, a burger, and a Coke. I ate as I tooled south down Mopac Expressway toward the Double Eagle Bar and Grill. I hoped to visit with the bartender who worked the shift when the brief fight occurred between Hastings and Packard.

The expressway was packed, which was no surprise. I have no idea how many vehicles race up and down those lanes everyday, but if I had a penny for each one, I'd be rich.

I hung in the outside lane at a steady sixty miles an hour, steering with one hand and eating my fries and burger with the other as the other drivers zoomed past.

Suddenly, the shriek of metal deafened me, and my pickup jerked to the right, bounced over the shoulder, and shot down a thirty-degree grassy incline. I dropped the burger and grabbed the wheel with both hands, at the same time slamming on my brakes.

Cars and trucks jammed the access road toward which I was hurtling. There was no room for me to fit in. I was about ten seconds away from slamming into the side of an eighteen-wheeler cattle truck. I stomped the brakes harder and spun the steering wheel to the left, hoping the pickup wouldn't flip. As the rear end skidded into a one-eighty the Silverado shuddered to a halt mere inches from the access road as the cattle truck roared past with an angry blast from his ear-splitting klaxon horn.

I dropped my forehead to the steering wheel and breathed a short prayer. The door jerked open.

"Hey, buddy. Are you okay? You hurt?"

When I managed to focus my eyes, two worried young men were staring at me.

"I thought you was a goner," one said.

I tried to laugh, but all I could do was croak, "I did too." I shook my head slowly. "I don't know what happened."

The other man pointed to the expressway. "A car up there ran into you. They knocked you off the road."

"Yeah," the other chimed in, "it was kind of dark red, you know, maroon. Looked like a couple of Chinese guys in it. We stopped to see if you was okay before we thought to get their license number."

"Looked to me like they did it on purpose," remarked the second one.

At that moment, an Austin P. D. cruiser pulled up, over-heads flashing.

For the next thirty minutes, we went over and over the incident. The cops took notes for their report, chalking it up as an accidental sideswipe.

"If it was an accident," I asked. "Why didn't they stop?"

"Look, Mr. Boudreaux," the young officer explained. "He's probably one of those dipsticks with a dozen war-rants out for him. He can't afford to stop."

I disagreed with his assessment, but I kept quiet. I just wanted to get on my way.

When I looked at the side of my pickup, I almost cried. My brand new Silverado, only three months old, now sported an ugly dent streaked with maroon paint in the side of the driver's door.

As I pulled back onto Mopac, I came to the sobering conclusion that someone wanted Bobby Packard to die, and not just the state of Texas.

Chapter Thirteen

The middle of the afternoon is usually a slow time for restaurants and bars, even an upscale bar and eatery like the Double Eagle on Austin's south side. On the lobby wall, a mural of two bald eagles, wings spread, talons extended, ready to claw its victim, greeted me. Through a large arched door to the right was the dining area. To the left was the bar.

Two men sat on stools at the end of the bar, heads together. The bartender, a tall, slender man with the long fingers of a pianist nodded to me. "Yes, sir. What'll it be?"

I climbed on a stool and eyed the enticing collection of liquor on the sideboard behind the bar. After the incident out on Mopac, I was sorely tempted to steady my nerves with two or three stiff shots of Jim Beam Black Label, but instead I simply grinned. "I've got me a problem, and I need help. Lots of help."

"You've come to the right place."

"Truth is, I'm looking for the bartender who worked here ten years ago. And to make it doubly difficult, I don't even know his name."

He nodded sympathetically. "Yep. I'd say you got a problem."

"Have you been here long?"

"Six years, but the old boy I work with, Pop Wingate, he's has been here since the Garden of Eden." He grinned and chuckled. "For an old man in his eighties, he's something else."

I forgot about the sideswipe. "Great. How can I get in touch with him?"

"He comes in a 6:00 tonight."

The clock on the wall read 3:30. "I'd sure like to talk to him now. Is there anyway I can get his home number?"

He flexed his long fingers. "I don't give out phone numbers, but tell you what. I'll call him, and let you talk to him. Okay?"

I grinned. "That'll work for me."

Five minutes later, I headed east for Airport Boulevard.

Twenty minutes later, I knocked on the door of apartment 129 at the Airport Towers Complex, trying to imagine an eighty-plus-year-old bartender.

The door opened, and Pop Wingate invited me in for what was going to be a revelation in more ways than one.

To say I was surprised when I saw him was an understatement of the same magnitude as calling Noah's flood a passing shower. Astonished probably fits the moment better, for from the top of his shiny baldhead to the rubber flip-flops on his feet, Pop Wingate was an amiable eighty-something in the body of a forty-year-old. Tan as Louisiana swamp water, he wore sweats and a tank top.

"Tony Boudreaux?" He extended his hand.

Still speechless, I took it, "That's . . . me." I shook his hand, marveling as his firm grip. "You're Pop Wingate?"

He grinned, and from that grin I could tell he took delight in the bewilderment scribbled across my face. Instinctively, I knew I was not the first person to stare gape-mouthed at him. "In the flesh." He stepped back. "Come in, come in. Would you care for some refreshment, tea, beer, water?" He gestured to the couch next to one wall.

Sitting, I declined his offer of refreshment, unable to get over how youthful he appeared, how tight his skin was, how few wrinkles he had. Resisting the impulse to grill him about his discovery of the fountain of youth, I admitted. "This might be a wild goose chase, Mr. Wingate."

"Call me Pop, and if it is a wild goose chase, so be it."

"Ten years or so back, there was a fight in the Double Eagle."

He laughed. "Not just ten years ago, son."

I laughed with him. "I can imagine. Anyway, this particular fight involved Albert Hastings. At the time he was governor-elect. He got into a fight with a man named—"

Pop cut me off. "Bobby Packard."

For the second time in as many minutes, I was at a loss for words. Finally, I managed to stammer out. "You knew him—them?"

The amiable smile fled his face. He aged twenty years. "Yeah, I knew them. But the fight you're talking about, I didn't see. I wish I had, but my shift ended before it happened. My partner Billy Ruiz saw it."

I grimaced. "What about him? Is he still around?"

Pop shook his head. "No. He died five or six years ago. It's a shame too. Billy was a nice guy. George—that's the skinny bartender you talked to earlier—took his place."

I shook my head. "Just my luck."

"Not necessarily," the older man said, a mischievous glint in his eyes. "Billy saw the fight, and if he told me about it once, he told it a hundred times. Believe it or not, I have the entire fight memorized blow by blow, not that there were that many punches thrown."

His reply buoyed my hopes. I leaned forward. "What happened?"

"According to Billy, it wasn't much of a fight. Bobby Packard was at the bar. He was a good customer. Never bothered anyone, never caused any problems, and he was always quick with a joke. Well, sir, according to Billy, Albert Hastings and another man in a suit came out of the dining room. Hastings was really plastered, and when he saw Bobby, he cursed and took a swing from the back."

His face darkened. "That was the kind of no-account Hastings was—hitting from behind. He hit Bobby on the shoulder, knocked him to the floor. Hastings cursed and kicked Bobby. Bobby jumped up and busted Hastings in the face and sent him sprawling. The other guy backed away, holding his hands up like he didn't want to fight." Pop drew a deep breath and released it noisily. "And that's all there was to it, such as it was." He paused, then added. "Personally, I'd have given a week's pay to see Hastings get what was coming to him."

I arched a single eyebrow. "So, I take it you didn't care for Hastings."

His eyes turned cold. "No. Hastings—" he paused and looked up at the ceiling, searching for words. Finally, he dropped his gaze back to me. "I don't know if Bobby killed him or not, but the man deserved what he got. He treated those around him like second-class citizens, good enough only to wipe his boots. I had heard a lot about him. I don't have any hard proof, but if even a third of what I heard was right, he deserved a seat at the right hand of old Satan himself."

"Such as?"

He shrugged. "Like I said, I don't have no proof."

"Tell me anyway."

"You name it. Bribe money from contractors; carrying on with other women; drugs." He eyed me keenly. "Tell you what. Get in touch with Sally Reston. She was one of the girls who hung around there back then. She had a few dates with Albert Hastings."

I jotted her name. "Dates?"

"Yeah, you know. She worked the bar. Classy gal, never caused no trouble."

"She still over there?"

"Naw. Age caught up with her, and the young eighteen-year-olds got her business. She was a decent girl though. Last I heard she was running a day care center for kids somewhere between Round Rock and Georgetown north of here."

I arched an eyebrow.

Pop chuckled. "Like they say, truth is stranger than fiction."

He was right about that. After all, fiction has to make sense. "What about Packard? Did you know him well?"

With a shrug, he replied. "As well as you could a customer. He was a hard worker, but like most young men, he was sowing his wild oats. That's how he met Hastings' wife, ah—" He stammered, trying to remember.

"Lorene," I said.

"Yeah, Lorene. That's it." He tapped the heel of his hand lightly against his forehead. "Memory's going. It must be getting old."

With a wry grin, I looked him up and down. "There might be some things you need to worry about, Pop, but getting old sure doesn't look like it's one of them. What's your secret? You look better than I do."

He chuckled. "Work hard, be honest, eat right, exercise every day, and have three fingers of bourbon before bedtime every night."

I looked around the neat apartment. "Are you married?"

Beaming, he nodded emphatically. "To the prettiest little twenty-one-year-old you've ever seen. I can tell you this, she's sure a handful." He paused, watching me intently as I stammered and stuttered for a response.

"Did—did you say twenty-one?"

He patted his bald head. "Like the old saying, son, figuratively speaking, there might be snow on the roof, but there's fire in the furnace."

For the third time since I arrived, I was speechless.

Suddenly, he broke into laughter. "Not really, son. I was joshing you." He grew solemn. "I was married though, to a wonderful woman. She's been gone now thirty-two years. I still wear my ring. I talk to her all the time. At night before I drop off to sleep, and in the mornings." A tear gathered in the corner of one eye. "I'll never forget her."

I glanced at his left hand. A simple silver band glittered on his finger. Rising slowly, I offered him my hand. "Thanks, Pop. You've made this a day I won't forget."

Chapter Fourteen

Sitting behind the wheel of my Silverado, I jotted more notes on my cards. For the third time in the last two days, I had been told that Bobby Packard was not one to initiate any confrontations. The first was from Bobby himself, then Lorene Hastings, and now, Pop Wingate.

In my job, I strive to be nonjudgmental and impartial, but the scales of my own personal sense of justice were beginning to tilt in Bobby Packard's favor.

Now, I'm not too sharp with cell phones. All I know is when they ring, I answer, then punch off at the conclusion of the conversation. I didn't want it to ring while I was interviewing Pop Wingate, so I had left it on the seat of my pickup. When I picked it up to check my messages, I saw that Landreth had called. I played back the call. "Mr. Boudreaux, Packard is innocent, I have documentation pointing to those responsible for Albert's death. Give me a call."

I immediately dialed his number, but all I got was busy signal. Muttering a curse, I yanked the pickup into gear and headed for Marble Falls. When I hit Loop 360, I tried again. Still busy. I called the operator and asked her to see if there were a conversation on the line.

Cold chills raced up my back when she reported the number was out of order.

An hour later, I pulled into an Easy Come, Easy Go convenience store on the outskirts of Marble Falls and asked for directions to Landreth's place. The clerk, who had been speaking with a lanky rancher wearing a straw hat, squinted at me at first with a dumbfounded, then suspicious glint in his eyes. "You a friend of his?"

I was sorely tempted to tell him it was none of his business, but I wanted directions, not problems. "Never met the man, but I have a appointment with him."

The rancher drawled, "Well, his place is five or six miles out on Farm Road 301, but I'm afraid you're too late, mister. Don Landreth is dead."

Stunned, I could only stare at him. Was this some kind of cowboy joke on the city boy? "When? I just heard from him a hour or so back."

The clerk shook his head slowly in dismay. "We just got word ourselves."

"What happened?"

"Don't know for sure. Lonnie—that's Sheriff Cobb's deputy—stopped in and said one of Landreth's people found him in the den with a bullet hole in his head. 'Pears he killed himself."

I just stared at him. Slowly the wheels in my head started turning. I had been so close . . . but, the proof of which Landreth had spoken could still be in his house. I knew I was grasping at straws. Maybe I could explain my predicament to his family. Maybe someone would be willing to help me search for the proof. Maybe.

"Did he have a wife and family?"

The lanky cowboy shook his head. "Nope. Bachelor. 'Course, he had house guests, but they only stayed overnight." He and the store clerk grinned lecherously at each other.

I cursed all the way back to Austin, wondering desperately just what evidence Landreth had possessed that could have cleared Bobby Packard.

As I drove, a tiny kernel of suspicion pushed aside some of the random thoughts tumbling about in my head. Landreth's sudden death seemed too timely to be mere coincidence. I glanced at my watch when I hit Mopac Expressway. It was almost 6:30.

If I hurried, I could visit Sally Reston north of Round Rock and still pick up Janice by 9:00.

Normally, I don't use my cell phone when I drive, but I was pressed for time. I pulled into the outside lane and dropped my speed to fifty-five.

There was no Sally Reston listed in information, but luck smiled on me. There was a Reston Day Care listed.

I didn't expect an answer because of the lateness of the hour, but I crossed my fingers that some hapless parent might have been unavoidably detained and the day care was still open.

No such luck. There was no answer, only voice mail. I decided not to leave a message.

Swinging off Mopac onto Research Boulevard, I cut north on Lamar, then a few blocks later, left on Peyton Gin Road. I was exhausted. The day had been long, but fortunately it had been profitable enough to reinforce my belief that Bobby Packard was telling the truth.

Mentally, I ticked off what I had learned in the last three days. First, there was the alleged video of an Asian making the hit on Hastings; second, the slugs taken from Hastings turned up missing before the rifling could be matched to Packard's Glock; third, Hastings initiated the slugfest at the Double Eagle; fourth, from both Lorene Hastings and Pop Wingate, I heard that Hastings was a politician gone bad; fifth, Don Landreth claimed he had evidence clearing Packard; sixth, Landreth died with a slug in his head.

I hesitated, considering the maroon automobile that had run me off the freeway. Accident? Or warning? Then there was the threatening message on my phone and the next day the blowout that sent Janice and me skidding off the road. Counting those incidents, I had nine reasons to believe Packard.

My cell phone rang. It was Jack Edney. "Tony. Buddy. What about it? You going to be my campaign manager?"

I thought of Don Landreth. "No way, Jack. No way at all." I punched off, then turned off the cell phone.

Chapter Fifteen

"What the—" was my first reaction as I passed Laurel Grove Road and spotted a red SUV in my driveway. Then I closed my eyes and groaned. It was Diane, my ex. I had forgotten all about her. She was due in town today. And tonight was the Halloween party with Janice. Perfect timing, I told myself wryly.

Diane rose from the couch and smiled brightly when I opened the door. Her voice was animated. "Hey, Tony. I hope you don't mind, but your landlord let me in." She held out her arms.

"Not a bit," I replied, reluctantly giving her a brief hug, knowing she was probably expecting me to spend the evening, maybe even the night, with her.

Frantically, I sought some way to extricate myself from the confusion. Trying to buy time, I stepped back and looked her up and down. She wore black slacks with a white blouse. She had cut her brown hair short, an attractive complement to her deep tan. "You look great."

She blushed and patted her hair. "You always knew how to flatter a woman."

76

I headed for the kitchen, still unable to decide what to do. "Something to drink? Coffee, soft drink, club soda, beer?"

A tiny frown knit her brows. "Beer? You told me back in Vicksburg you were on the wagon. You know, A. A."

Opening the refrigerator, I grabbed a Diet Coke. "I am, but there's some Old Milwaukee a friend left."

"Sounds good," she replied, still standing in front of the couch.

I handed it to her and nodded to the couch. I remained standing. I didn't want to suggest anything by sitting next to her. "So, how was the trip?"

"Boring." She took a sip of Old Milwaukee. "Am I glad to be here. I almost got lost a couple times. This town sure has grown since we started college here. How long ago was that, twenty years or so?"

With a shake of my head, I replied. "Hard to believe, huh? Just you wait until you start driving around."

She looked up at me seductively. "Whenever you're ready."

I gulped. The look in her eyes promised more, much more than I wanted. And it wasn't driving around.

They say God looks after fools and children. Well, he must have been looking after me for at that very moment, the doorbell rang.

It was Jack Edney, the friend who, though he had become a multi-millionaire, was still a pain in the neck. And he was here to pressure me into taking on the monumental task of managing his campaign for city council. But at that moment, I had never been so tickled to see him. I yanked open the door.

Jack blurted out. "Now listen to me before you say no, Tony. I—"

"Jack! Buddy! Come on in. There's someone here I want you to meet." I grabbed his hand and dragged him inside.

He jerked back, but I clutched his hand with a grip that only death could tear loose. "Hey, what's going on? What—" Then he spotted Diane. He stopped resisting, and a broad smile leaped to his lips, splitting his round face. He still wore his hair in a burr. His head reminded me of a bowling ball.

I made the introductions. "Jack, this is the young lady I called you about last night, Diane Mays. And Diane, this is Jack. You two have something in common. Jack is W. R's brother."

Her eyes widened in surprise, and Jack shot me a puzzled look. "Diane is from Vicksburg, Jack. She's acquainted with W. R."

She glanced at me, aware that I had said *acquainted* instead of *dated*. I winked at her. She understood. "Pleased to meet you, Jack." She stepped forward and held out her hand.

Forgetting all about his altruistic desire to make Austin a safer place for the children, Jack stumbled over himself to take her hand and delivered the classic line. "Talk about a small world."

Diane nodded demurely.

"So, you know W. R.?"

Glancing fleetingly at me, she replied, "Yes. We met a few times—business, you know."

He took a shot at being charming. "Well, I'm the good-looking brother."

She nodded briefly. "I can see that."

Jack blushed furiously.

I suppressed a wry grin, knowing she would never reveal the fact she and W. R. had been two sides of a love triangle. And from the look on her face, I guessed she was strongly contemplating comparing one brother to the other.

Like a love-struck boy, Jack stood transfixed, holding

her hand while I explained. "After your call yesterday, Diane, I contacted Jack. He owns a nice apartment complex out on Highway 290."

"Oh, really?"

"That's the road to Johnson City, which will make it a convenient commute for you." I turned to Jack. "Diane is with the National Park Service."

Jack nodded, mesmerized by her beaming smile. "That's nice," was all he said.

"Her last assignment was the battlefield in Vicksburg."

I didn't think it possible, but Jack's smile grew wider. "That's nice."

"She was transferred to Johnson City."

Jack nodded again, keeping his eyes on Diane. "That's really nice."

"One of the homes where President Johnson once lived," she said, her own eyes fixed on Jack.

"That's nice," he said once again.

"I'm anxious to see it," Diane said.

Jack nodded. "That's nice." He continued to stare at her for another moment until he realized what he had said. "I mean, I'd like to see the house too," he mumbled, his eyes still locked on hers.

Witty repartees obviously were not one of Jack's strong suits, so I did what I could to help out. "Jack, why don't you take Diane out to the complex and show her the apartment. No sense in wasting time. She might want to move in tonight." I smiled inwardly at my deft maneuvering.

Without looking at me, Diane gushed. "I think that would be absolutely wonderful, that is, if you don't mind, Mr. Edney."

"Not a bit, not a bit." Jack gushed back. "And call me Jack."

She smiled coquettishly. "All right, Jack, but you have to call me Diane."

Suddenly I was jealous. I had made every effort to dump her on Jack, but now she had dropped me like the proverbial hot potato. Hold on, Tony, I reminded myself. That was what you wanted. On the other hand if that were so, why did I feel as if I had been jilted?

They headed for the door, eyes still fixed on each other. Not even looking in my direction, Diane said, "Thanks, Tony. See you later."

I had the distinct impression that the remark was simply an afterthought. I was nothing more that the period at the end of the sentence.

Jack confirmed my feelings. Without looking at me, he mumbled over his shoulder, "I owe you, buddy."

I watched as she climbed into his Cadillac, leaving her SUV in my driveway.

Chapter Sixteen

Janice had dressed as Little Bo Peep in black pumps, long white stockings, a billowing dress, lacy bonnet, and pigtails. A shepard's staff topped off the ensemble. I was decked out in a devil's outfit, replete with two horns and a pitchfork.

We tucked into her little Miata, but neither her staff nor my pitchfork would fit inside with the top up, and the weather was too chilly to ride with a window down.

Grudgingly, she accepted the fact that she was reduced to riding to the party in my Silverado. I tried to pacify her. "A lot of the folks at the party drive pickups. No one will notice."

"I will," she replied with a petulant curl to her lips.

"I'll bet Nora Charles wouldn't mind," I said, teasing her.

"I'm not Nora Charles," she snapped.

I shook my head. Poor little rich girl. If anyone ever tries to convince you that money—piles of money—could never spoil you, don't believe him. In all fairness, Janice did try to fit in with the masses.

Once we drove off, the first subject she broached was Diane.

Making a concerted effort to appear blasé about the whole matter, I explained what had taken place and added, "She and Jack seemed attracted to each other."

"Good!" she sniffed. "Maybe she'll leave you alone."

Downtown, we turned off I-35 onto the access road. The Hotel Chateaubriand was on the corner of Fifth and Congress.

The corners of Fifth, Sixth, and Seventh Streets and the access road were the gathering spots for homeless, vacant-eyed winos and tattered itinerants scrabbling for coins to purchase another bottle of Thunderbird wine.

In the mornings they waited for contractors looking for day workers. At night they panhandled cars stopped at the light signals.

We hit a green light, and as I turned onto Fifth, I gave a cursory glance at a small cluster of dirty men standing under a street light. They all looked the same, pinched faces, hollow eyes, and patched clothes that hung from withered bodies. I shivered, wondering how they could tolerate such a life.

Half a block past the huddle of winos, one of the faces suddenly exploded in my head. My old man! John Roney Boudreaux! One of the winos looked exactly like him.

I cut sharply at the next corner.

Janice looked around at me in alarm. "Tony! What on earth are you doing?"

"Nothing. I saw something back there I want to take another look at."

"What? There was nothing back there but those horrid winos. What—" she stopped abruptly. With a tone of disbelief, she asked, "Do you think—" She pressed her fingers to her lips.

Janice had accompanied me to our family reunion the previous year on Whiskey Island in Atchafalaya Swamp where she had met my father, who as usual stayed drunk the entire three days, not even sobering up when he stole my laptop.

"I don't know if it was my old man or not. I didn't get a real good look. It wouldn't surprise me though. You remember, he was here in town a couple years back. It's been over a year since I saw him. As far as I know," I added with resignation, "he could be dead, or he could show up on my front porch tonight." I circled the block, but by the time we made it back to Fifth Street, the small cluster of men had vanished into the dark alleyways and shadows of dumpsters filled with garbage.

Chapter Seventeen

As with any social affair that Janice condescends to attend, the Halloween affair at the Chateaubriand was a gala event of bright lights, haute cuisine, enough alcohol to float a city, and spirited music by which ghosts and goblins could dance the night away.

I wish I could say we won prizes for the best costumes, but that coveted award went to a couple dressed in a caricature of the old farmer and his spinster daughter in the classic painting, *American Gothic.*

During the gala, Beatrice Morrison, CEO of Chalk Hills Distillery and number one in Austin's social register, sidled up to me as I ladled spiked punch into two cups. "Hello, Tony. How good of you to come." Honey dripped from her words.

I'd been around her enough to know when she was setting me up. "Thank you, Mrs. Morrison. I'm pleased to be here." My words were just as honeyed.

"Oh, Tony, you know me better than that. Call me Beatrice."

Holding the full cups, I turned to face her. "All right—Beatrice."

She laid her hand on my forearm the way society people do when they're going to spread a piece of choice gossip. "Janice is always bragging on your Cajun dishes." Her brows knit slightly. "Would it be too much of an imposition to ask you to bring a container of—I think she called it court bouillon—to my reception day after tomorrow? We'll have a silver serving dish for it."

"Catfish court bouillon?"

"Yes that's it. I couldn't remember the name," she replied in a tone that suggested the word *catfish* was not in her social lexicon.

What could I say? I wasn't flattered because I knew she was asking just to please her niece who had come to love French cuisine, especially those dishes with a Cajun flair. "No problem at all, Mrs.—I mean, Beatrice. Will five gallons be enough? That's the largest pot I have."

She smiled brightly. "Splendid."

"But," I added, stopping her as she turned to depart, "I might not be able to stay for the entire reception. I'd like to," I said, "but I have work to do."

If possible, her smile grew brighter. "Too bad. We'll miss you."

Sometime during the Halloween gala, a slow rain began, a cold drizzle that penetrated to the bone. I left Janice at the front door of her condo around one o'clock with the promise to pick her up at eight. She wanted to play Nick and Nora Charles again.

"Dress warmly," I warned her. "Tomorrow looks like it'll be a miserable day."

The drizzle remained steady. Oncoming headlights reflected off the shiny roads, creating a blinding glare, and in the rain, the asphalt pavement seemed to disappear. As I headed north on Lamar, I spotted a soaked figure on the shoulder of the road. His hat pulled down and the collar of his coat drawn tight about his neck, he hunched his head and shoulder into the rain.

For a moment, I considered giving him a lift, but compassion gave way to wisdom and I drove on.

To my relief, my driveway was empty. "Good," I muttered, parking the Silverado under the carport, relieved that Diane was out of my life. I shivered as I climbed out. "This night is not fit for man or beast," I mumbled. As the words rolled off my lips, I remembered the solitary figure trudging along the side of the road.

The chiming of the doorbell pulled me from a sound sleep at 2:40 A.M. I lay motionless for a moment, thinking I had dreamed the doorbell, but then the chiming rolled down the dark hall and into the bedroom again.

"Who the . . ." I mumbled as I swung my legs over the side of the bed and flipped on the night-light. I slipped into my robe and house shoes and groggy with sleep, padded to the door.

The bell rang again just as I flipped on the porch light. I peered through the viewer. All I could see was the top of a soggy hat, and then the hat tilted back. My eyes popped wide. I couldn't believe it. To quote Yogi Berra, "Déjà vu all over again."

I opened the door and stared at my old man, John Roney Boudreaux. He tried to focus his bloodshot eyes on me. "This Tony Boudreaux's place?" he croaked.

Filled with mixed emotions, I stared at him. I nodded slowly. "Hello, John." I couldn't call him Pa, not after Whiskey Island.

He rubbed a dirty fist in his sunken eyes and squinted up at me. "Tony? I didn't recognize you, boy."

Stepping back from the door, I motioned for him to come inside. "Come on in where it's warm." There was no feeling in my voice.

He staggered inside, clutching an almost empty bottle of wine in his hand. The rain had disintegrated the paper bag in which he had carried the bottle. The only remnant of the bag was the collar of paper under the bony hand grasping the neck of the wine bottle.

Water dripped from him, soaking the carpet. I took his elbow. "Come on into the kitchen."

He didn't resist.

I gave him a chair at the table. I didn't mind water on the tile floor.

He plopped down and promptly took another drink.

Making an effort to suppress the anger suddenly boiling in my veins, I said, "I'm surprised to see you after the family reunion at Whiskey Island last year."

"Reunion? What reunion?" his slurred reply was barely intelligible.

"Summer of last year, at Whiskey Island," I snapped.

For several seconds, he looked up at me with glazed eyes. His tongue grew thicker, "Don't 'member no reunion."

I stared at him, a rain-soaked, withered drunk. My anger faded away, replaced by a weary indifference. "You're wet. I'll get a towel and dry clothes. Then I'll fix the couch for you."

My father nodded slowly and began disrobing in the middle of the kitchen.

Later, after he had passed out on the couch, I stood staring down at him, still expecting perhaps not a flood of emotion or feelings, but at least a tiny ripple. There was nothing.

Then I remembered the solitary figure in the rain. It was probably my old man. I tried to imagine the cold he must have felt. "No," I muttered, "he was probably too drunk to feel the cold."

With a deep sigh and a weary shake of my head, I padded back to the bedroom, not looking forward to what I was certain would be a sleepless night.

To my surprise, I eventually dozed for a couple hours, awakening to a dreary morning of cold drizzle and a father with no compunction whatsoever about stealing anything he could get his hands on.

I glanced at the clock: 6:15 A.M. No time to waste. I rolled out of bed and headed for the kitchen to put on the coffee. John Roney lay on his back, still as death, his mouth gaping open, snoring lightly.

What to do with him while I was gone? Leaving him alone in my apartment could very likely make me a candidate for accessory before and after the fact, whatever the fact might be. I knew exactly what he would do. He'd prowl through the apartment for anything to pawn. His major goal in life was the next bottle of cheap wine.

While drawing water for the Bunn coffeemaker, I decided on a course of action. Gathering all my valuables, I hauled them into the garage, after which I drove to the nearest convenience store and purchased a padlock and hasp, which I screwed to the door between the kitchen and garage. And I put it on the garage side, not the kitchen where he could pry it off. The garage door already had a padlock, preventive security for the Model T Runabout.

The only item worth pawning left in the house was the desktop computer, and I figured it was too heavy for him to carry.

I stared at myself in the mirror while shaving. I shook my head, wondering just what the world was coming to when a body had to hide valuables from his own father.

Before I pulled out, I fed Oscar who, for some reason or another, ignored the tiny flakes bobbing on the surface of the aquarium. "You'd better eat, little guy," I said. "Keep up your strength."

The little tiger barb was a real survivor, having weathered Jack's chemical attack as well as exceeding its life expectancy by almost two years. I touched the tip of my finger to the surface by his food, hoping to entice him to eat but he continued to swim in lazy circles through the plastic water sprite and Amazonian sword plants.

I went over my schedule for the day. First, I would look up Sally Reston and then L. D. Bryson, Bobby's supervisor at A. A. Aggregates. I hesitated, uncertain about Bryson. *Packard had admitted telling Bryson he wanted to kill Hastings. Maybe I should not waste my time on Bryson.*

I plopped down at the desktop computer. Behind me, my old man snored. My blood ran cold when I saw the date on the task bar, November 1. After today, only three days until Bobby's execution. I pushed the thought from my mind. I had work to do. I e-mailed Eddie Dyson, my savior on more than one occasion.

Austin's one-time resident stool pigeon, Eddie Dyson had become a computer whiz and wildly successful entrepreneur.

Instead of sleazy bars and greasy money, he had found his niche for snitching in the combination of computers and credit cards. Any information that I couldn't find, he could. There were only two catches if you dealt with Eddie. First, you never asked him how he did it; and second, he only accepted *Visa* credit cards for payment.

I never asked Eddie why he only accepted *Visa*. It seemed like any credit card should be sufficient, but considering the value of his service, I never posed the question. As far as I was concerned, if he wanted to be paid in Japanese yen, I'd pack up a half dozen bushels and send them to him.

Failure was not a word in his vocabulary. His services did not come cheap, but he produced. Sometimes the end is indeed worth the means.

In my e-mail, I asked for background checks on Lei Sun Huang, whom both Danny O'Banion and Joe Ray Burrus claimed headed up the Ying On triad; and Joey Soong, the top man in the Sing Leon tong. As an afterthought, I asked for the work history of Robert Packard at A. A. Aggregates in Austin, Texas, on the outside chance there was something there. And I added ASAP.

"You look terrible," Janice exclaimed when she climbed into the truck later that morning.

With a dry laugh, I shifted into gear and pulled into the traffic. "I had an early morning visitor."

She paused in the middle of buckling her seat belt. "You don't mean it!" she gasped.

"Want to bet?"

"So it *was* him you saw last night?"

"Probably."

She drew a deep breath and leaned back in the seat. "Did he have anything to say? I mean, about—" she hesitated.

"—stealing the laptop at the reunion?"

"Yes."

Stretching my fingers around the wheel, I grunted, "He doesn't even remember the reunion. He just came in, downed the rest of his Thunderbird, and passed out on the couch. He was still there when I left."

Janice remained silent, but I could hear the wheels turning.

I answered before she asked the question, "Don't worry. Anything he could pawn I locked in the garage with the Model T. Now, that doesn't mean he might not carry off the kitchen table or the microwave. At least, he'd have to work hard for that, and I really don't believe my old man would be willing to work hard for anything."

"Maybe not," she hesitated. "I know he's your father, and I don't want to hurt your feelings, Tony, but you better watch him closely."

With a chuckle, I agreed.

She looked out at the overcast sky. "I hope it clears off by tomorrow."

"For your aunt's reception?"

"That we can move inside. I want good weather so we can drive out in the little car."

I chuckled. When I bought Model T in Vicksburg, I knew Janice would fall in love with it, and she had. "You'd better cross your fingers."

"Don't worry."

"Where are we headed now?"

"North of Round Rock. Almost to Georgetown. A lady named Sally Reston."

"Who is she?"

I explained.

Janice looked around at me with a cryptic frown on her face. "You're kidding me. An ex-hooker running a day care center?"

"That's what the man said. I'm just taking it on faith."

Chapter Eighteen

The day care center was a tan metal building about the size of the local 7/11, closer to Georgetown than Round Rock. Inside it was bright and airy, the vividly painted walls decorated with cheerful images of various nursery rhymes and fairy tales. Along one wall, a laughing mouse ran up a clock. On another, a cat played a fiddle while a dog laughed as the cow jumped over the moon and the dish ran away with the spoon.

A older woman who appeared to be in her late fifties or early sixties was helping another woman herd a squiggly line of small children down the hall. Her brown hair was cut short, making her full face even fuller. She wore washed-out jeans and a bright red sweatshirt with the words, *Love the Little Children*, printed across the front. She looked around and smiled warmly, the kind of smile *Grandmère* Ola would give me, the kind all grandmothers give their grandchildren. "Can I help you folks?"

"Yes, Ma'am. I'm looking for Sally Reston."

"That's me. Let me help Mattie settle the children in for breakfast snacks, and I'll be right back."

As she disappeared down the hall, Janice leaned toward me and whispered, "She doesn't look like a hooker."

"Ex-hooker."

"Okay, ex-hooker."

"What's an ex-hooker supposed to look like?"

Janice shrugged.

"She's older than I expected," I muttered.

"What do you mean?"

"My Sally Reston worked the Double Eagle ten or eleven years ago. I figured she'd be in her early forties, not as old as this lady."

"Your Sally Reston?" she arched a questioning eyebrow.

I shrugged. "Figure of speech. Anyway, this can't be her. How many sixty-year-old hookers do you know?"

"Are you kidding? I don't know any hookers period."

Sally returned, brushing at a spot on her sweatshirt. With an amiable chuckle, she explained, "Milk. Little Georgie dribbles when he drinks." She chuckled and looked up. "Now, what can I do for you?"

I made the introductions. "I'm not sure I have the right Sally Reston, Ma'am, but do you happen to know a man by the name of Pop Wingate?"

The smile on her lips flickered, but remained, though it was not as cordial as a moment earlier. "Used to. Years ago."

I breathed a sigh of relief. Despite the age confusion, I had obviously found the right person. "If you don't mind, I'd like to talk to you about Albert Hastings."

The smile faded from her face completely, replaced by a frown on her lips and a suspicious gleam in her eyes. "You the cops?"

"No, Ma'am."

"Albert's dead," she replied in a flat voice. She glanced around to see if anyone was nearby. "Why should I talk to you?"

I turned on the charm. Smiling brightly, I took a step back, careful not to invade her space. "Like I said, Pop Wingate gave me your name. He said to tell you 'hi.'" The last was a lie, but it served the purpose I wanted.

A tiny smile replaced the frown on her face.

I continued, "I went to Pop in an effort to save a man from execution at Huntsville. He sent me to you. He thinks you might be able to help."

With a wary look in her eyes, she studied me a moment, then switched her gaze to Janice. "What do you want from me?"

"Same thing I wanted from Pop. To help save Bobby Packard," I replied simply.

She maintained an inscrutable expression on her face. Her eyes narrowed. "He was convicted. He got what he deserved."

"Maybe so. I won't argue with you, but will you at least tell me about Albert Hastings?" She studied me a moment longer, considering whether to talk to us or throw us out. Finally, she nodded to a closed door next to a wall mural of little Miss Muffett sitting on her tuffet. "My office is in there. No one will disturb us."

Inside, she indicated two chairs in front of her desk. "Please."

We sat.

Wearily, she slumped into her chair. "Up front, understand, I don't want any publicity. I can't afford any. Guarantee that or I won't say a word."

"You don't need to worry about that, Miss Reston. Truth is, unless you were an eyewitness to the murder, you'll never be involved. I'm just trying to find out more about Hastings. Maybe I can find some other avenues to explore."

She looked around the office. "I've worked hard these last ten years to build a nice little business here. I have a good reputation in the community. I want to keep it."

"You'll have no problems with me," I said, "I promise."

With a groan of resignation she said, "I had hoped I was finished with Albert and the Double Eagle," she sighed, "but, I don't suppose you can ever get away from your past. You know something, Mr. Boudreaux. I've learned there is no such thing as starting over in life. It's really about picking up the pieces and just going on. The past, regardless of how good or bad, is still your past. You just suck it up and keep going."

I nodded, leaning forward slightly. "Pop said you had dates with Hastings."

"Yes, several, until I found out just how despicable a man he was. He put me in the hospital with his fists. That's when I dropped him and the whole business." Her eyes blazed fire. "He was a cruel egomaniac. He thought he was better than everyone and treated everyone that way. Oh, but the man loved to party, I'll say that for him." She stared defiantly at Janice. "We all did. There was nothing Albert didn't try—that *we* didn't try—drugs included. His favorite was coke."

"Where did he get it?"

She laughed caustically. "From his politician pal, Samuel Jefferson Bradford."

"Bradford!" I looked at Janice in disbelief.

Sally gave me a wry grin. "Yep. Texas' very own distinguished Democratic senator." She laughed bitterly. "Albert was a world-class hypocrite. He hated Bradford. Told me so several times, yet he refused to break away. Maybe it was the drugs. I don't know."

"Why did he hate him?"

She shrugged, "He never said."

"Did Hastings ever mention anything about his wife and Bobby Packard having an affair?"

She snorted, "Lordy, that man didn't have room to talk. But, to answer your question, no. He never talked about his wife."

"What about Bradford? Do you have any idea where he got his drugs?"

Pursing her lips, she shook her head. "No, but more than once, he showed up at a party with a Chinese dude. Back then, the Chinks supplied drugs to a lot of people. I don't know about now."

"Can you remember anyone else who came to your parties?"

She pondered the question. "Not really. Well, maybe once or twice Hastings' campaign manager and some of his assistants showed up. Not often. The parties were really just for the big wheels."

"Campaign manager? You're talking about Don Landreth."

"Yeah, and his assistant, Eric Lavern."

"Lavern?"

"Yes. He must have been sewn to Landreth's coattail. They were always together."

"Is he still around?"

She shrugged again. "Beats me."

"Did you know Bobby Packard?"

"I met him. Seemed like an okay guy. We never had any dates, if that's what you mean."

I didn't get as much as I had hoped from her, but I did pick up enough to fill a couple holes and open up a few more. Bradford, whom Sally claimed Hastings hated, supplied the drugs. Could the Chinaman have been his supplier? And then there was Eric Lavern. Maybe he knew Landreth's secret. The next problem was to find him.

I rose and thanked Sally Reston.

She nodded. "Remember. No publicity." She gave Janice a wan smile. "You'll understand this, Honey. I've had a hard life. I'm almost forty. I don't have time to start over."

Chapter Nineteen

Back in the truck, Janice looked up at me in disbelief. "Did you hear what she said? She isn't even forty."

"I heard," I said, jotting notes on my cards. I glanced at her. "Like she said, turning tricks is a hard life."

Janice studied me thoughtfully. "Do all of them age like she has? I mean, hookers?"

I shrugged. "Probably. Alcohol, drugs, and all-night parties don't lend themselves to a healthy life-style according to any survey I've read." I dropped the cards back in my shirt pocket and started the pickup. "Of course, there might be one tomorrow saying they are."

She grimaced and shook her head. "I doubt it. Now what?"

I handed her my cell phone. "See if there's a number for Eric Lavern."

"Only two Laverns. A. Lavern and Cory Lavern," she announced minutes later.

"We'll stop somewhere and look up the addresses."

"Why not just call them?"

"Because, detective, they can't brush you off as easily face-to-face."

"Oh."

After entering the city limits of Round Rock, I spotted a sign pointing toward Brushy Creek. On impulse I took the exit. "Have you ever seen the round rock?" I kept my eyes on the road.

Janice frowned. "Round rock?"

"Yeah, the one the town was named for. It's in the middle of the creek down in a gully. It isn't really round. More oval shaped than round. It's where the old Chisholm Trail forded Brushy Creek."

She looked at me quizzically. "How do you know so much about it?"

I turned left onto a narrow road that descended sharply to the creek below. "Read about it once just after Mom and I came to Austin. I wondered if it was still here, so I drove out to see for myself." I gestured to the burgeoning city about us. "Twenty years ago, there wasn't much out here, so it was easy to find. Hey, there it is."

The dry-weather bridge spanning the creek was only a couple feet above the water. A few feet east of the bridge was the round rock in the middle of the creek. Some forty-five or fifty inches in diameter, it rose three feet out of the water. Some prankster had painted it chartreuse.

"Now, you can say you've seen the round rock."

With a wry grin, she replied. "Great way to start up a conversation. 'Hey, guess what I did the other day. I saw the round rock.' That will be a big hit at the monthly meeting of my Daylily Club."

As we approached the Austin city limits, I pulled into a Shell service station and looked up Lavern in the directory.

Moments later, we were back on the road heading for Braker Street. We turned south off Braker onto Bluff Bend Drive.

The house was in a middle-class neighborhood. I parked in front of 4396 Bluff Bend. A. Lavern. I studied the house, a one-story red brick with a Gothic porch supported by antebellum columns—typical modern Texas architecture. The grass needed mowing, and the trim, painting.

"I'll check," I told Janice, climbing out.

I knocked on the door.

No answer.

I tried again.

Still no answer.

Drapes covered the windows so I couldn't peer inside.

Maybe I ought to try the back, I told myself, but just before I stepped off the porch, the door opened. "Good morning," I said brightly.

The woman behind the screen eyed me warily. Even through the gauzy door screen, I could tell she was a tired woman, probably tired from working more hours than she could handle, tired from worry, just tired.

"Don't worry, Ma'am. I'm not selling anything or taking a survey," I joked.

She nodded, still remaining silent.

"Miss A. Lavern?"

"*Ms.* Lavern," she said, correcting me.

"Alice?"

"Arlene."

"Thanks. Ms. Lavern, I'm trying to run down a man named Eric Lavern. Would you happen to know him?"

Her eyes narrowed in suspicion. "Maybe."

My hopes surged. Maybe meant yes. I continued, "Years back, he worked as an assistant campaign manager for Albert Hastings. I had a couple questions he might be able to answer for me."

She pursed her lips. "You the cops?"

"No, Ma'am." Briefly, I explained what I was doing. "Eric worked with Don Landreth, but—"

"Why don't you ask Landreth then?" she demanded.

I grimaced. "He died yesterday."

The announcement cut through the defensive posture she had put up. Her eyes grew wide in disbelief, and she pressed one hand against her lips. Tears welled in her eyes. She gasped. "D-Don? Don Landreth is dead?" her voice trembled.

"Yes, Ma'am. I had an appointment to visit with him yesterday about 5:00. I learned about his passing when I reached Marble Falls." I hoped she wouldn't ask how he died.

Her tears overflowed onto her weathered cheeks. She wiped her eyes with the tips of her fingers. "He was a good man. I'm sorry for him. He helped us over some hard times after that no-good husband of mine deserted us."

"Eric Lavern is your husband?"

"Was," she snapped.

"I see. Can you tell me where he is?"

She shook her head slowly. Bitterly, she replied, "He left me and kids six or seven years ago. I divorced him. 'He needed more in life than we could offer' he told me, and then he left." Her eyes narrowed, and she used several very descriptive and uncomplimentary expletives to describe Eric and his ancestry.

Disappointment flooded over me.

She continued, "I haven't seen him since he left, but last year, a friend claimed she saw him working the bar at Frio's on Sixth Street. You might ask down there." She paused. "Is he in some kind of trouble?"

I could hear a trace of hope in her voice. I replied, "I don't know."

A slow, bitter smile played over her thin lips. "I hope

so. I hope he hurts like we hurt." Her words trembled with anger.

For a moment, I hesitated. "Ms. Lavern, I hate to dredge up old memories, but do you happen to have a picture of Eric?"

For a moment, I thought she would refuse. "I'll be right back."

When she returned, she slipped an 8×10 photograph between the screen door and the doorjamb. "Here. I don't want it."

"Thanks." I looked at the picture, and at that moment, I truly knew the depth of the hatred she carried for Eric Lavern. She had given me their wedding picture.

When I climbed back in the pickup, I winked at Janice. "We got lucky. Now it's Sixth Street."

With a curl of her lips, she said, "Sixth Street? Isn't that were all the saloons and bordellos are?"

I leaned over and touched my lips to hers. "Welcome to the life of a detective, Mrs. Charles."

Chapter Twenty

Back on the I–35, we slipped into a lane of traffic and followed the leader. Keeping her eyes on the road ahead, Janice asked, "So, how do we stand after three and a half days?"

"A lot of *he said–she said* stuff, but nothing really substantial." I hadn't told her about the warning message or the sideswipe or the death of Don Landreth. "Most of what we have indicates Hastings deserved what he got, but there's nothing to prove Bobby didn't pull the trigger."

She looked around. "So, we aren't doing so well, huh?"

I didn't want to admit to her terse assessment, but in all honesty, she very succinctly summed up where we stood.

At 10:00 A.M., Sixth Street was just opening its eyes in snippets and snatches, in patches and parcels. The street awakened like a drunk with only two hours sleep, reluctant and recalcitrant.

Proprietors with bloodshot eyes growled, some quickly downing a slug of the hair of the dog to ease a searing headache. We went straight to Frio's, but the owner had never heard of Eric Lavern.

103

So, we started up one side of the seven-block district, hitting every bistro and bar, every club and cabaret, every tattoo parlor and tavern. Sixth Street doesn't cater to cops, PIs, or insurance adjusters, so our cover story was that Eric Lavern was a cousin we hadn't seen in years. His ex-wife, Arlene, sent us down here.

It was a simple story, but those work best for me, probably because I'm a simple person.

The first bar we entered was the Red Rabbit. Janice hesitated when the stench of sour beer and whiskey mixed with stale cigarette smoke hit us square in the face. She wrinkled her nose. "Ugh."

"Get used to it," I whispered. "It doesn't get any better."

We were met with suspicion at first, but as we told our story, most seemed to be willing to cooperate, although somewhat grudgingly. Several of them knew Eric, and some knew his ex-wife was named Arlene. That gave us a thin cloak of credibility.

Within an hour, we had finished the south side of Sixth Street.

Janice groaned, "I don't think we'll ever find him." She shivered. "I can't believe people frequent these—these—" She struggled to find the appropriate descriptor.

I laughed. "They do. Trust me." I paused at the curb. "Can't tell. Our luck might change over there," I said, pointing across the street to a saloon with the inspired name, The Hollow Leg.

The cabaret was locked. I knocked. No answer. Peering through the stained window, I spotted the bartender and gestured to the door. He shook his head.

I knocked and gestured once again.

Anger contorting his face, the bartender jerked open the door and glared at me. He was a tall, sallow-faced man who looked like he was mad at the world. As soon as I mentioned Eric Lavern, he exploded into curses.

"You bet I know that stinking slimeball. He cleans this place for me, that is, when the crud feels like it." He threw open the door and waved his hand at the dark interior of the bar. Empty beer cans and mugs littered the tabletops; ashtrays overflowed; and trash lay scattered across the floor. It was worse than when the cops toss an apartment. "See this mess? The jerk was supposed to be here at eight. I come in fifteen minutes ago, and here it is, a stinking mess. And look at the time. 11:00 A.M. I should be open now, but I got to keep the doors locked until I get this joint cleaned up."

One trick I learned when interviewing an irate citizen like the bartender was to let him rant until he cleared the bile from his system. When he calmed down, I pitched him our cover story, then added, "I can't blame you for being upset. Do you know if he lives around here somewhere?"

He eyed me narrowly. I could see the stubbornness in his face, the knit brows, lips pressed together. I had the feeling he knew where Eric lived, but he wasn't going to tell us. I had an idea. "Look, we haven't seen him in years, but he is family. Personally, my cousin here and I are embarrassed that one of our family would leave you in a lurch. If you'd give us some garbage bags, we'd be happy to clean off the tables for you. That would help some, wouldn't it?"

Beside me, I heard Janice gasp.

His eyes opened in surprise. "Hey, you'd do that?"

"Yes."

His eyes narrowed. He studied me suspiciously, then shook his head. "Why? It ain't your responsibility."

I felt Janice tugging on my sleeve. I didn't look around at her. "Maybe not, but I'd feel better. We'd both feel better," I said, emphasizing *both*.

Clearing her throat, Janice tugged harder on my sleeve.

"Wouldn't we, cousin," I said, smiling around at her.

Her eyes blazed fire, but she nodded and reluctantly replied, "Yes."

Shaking his head, he took a deep breath. "Well, if that don't beat all." A grin popped up on his lips. "Just scraping the cans and bottles off the tables and dumping the ashtrays in the bags would be a big help. At least I can unlock the doors then. I'll get the bags," he said, heading for the rear.

We followed him inside, and when he was out of earshot, Janice exclaimed. "Tony, what on earth have you done?" She looked around the room. "I'm not touching those filthy cans. Can you imagine who drank out of them?"

"Hey, you're the one who wanted to play Nick and Nora Charles," I reminded her. "You've got no choice. He knows where we can find Eric. I'm certain. Once we do this for him, he has to tell us."

"Why?" She glared up at me defiantly.

"*Quid pro quo*," I said. "*Quid pro quo*."

She frowned.

I explained. "Tit for tat. You wash my back; I'll wash yours."

She blew out through her carefully painted lips and eyed her manicured nails apprehensively. She arched an eyebrow. "All right, but you owe me."

In ten minutes, we had cleared the tables, knotted the bags, and I had helped the bartender deposit them out back in the alley.

He grinned at me. "Hey, pal, I appreciate the help. You didn't have to do all that for me. Come back inside, and I'll treat you to a beer."

"Thanks, I'm on the wagon, but like I said, I need to find my cousin. You don't have any idea where I could look, do you?"

He studied me a moment, then shrugged. "Why not? You did me a favor. See this alley? It runs seven blocks down to the access road to the Interstate. This is where Eric Lavern's been living for the last five years."

I rolled my eyes. Another John Roney Boudreaux. "Thanks."

We went out the front and circled the building to the alley. "Here we are," I announced.

Janice looked around and frowned. "Where?"

"Our pal the bartender said Eric lives in this alley."

Her eyes widened. "You've got to be kidding. There's nothing here but dumpsters and garbage."

"Maybe so. That means we have seven blocks of dumpsters and garbage to look through." I looked down at her with a crooked grin. "Well, are you up to it?"

She set her jaw. "If you can do it, so can I."

I could have married her at that moment.

We found Eric in a cardboard box behind a dumpster in the second block. He lay on his back sleeping, with only his head sticking out of the box. At first we weren't sure it was Eric and compared him to the wedding picture. If that pitiful excuse for a human was Eric Lavern, he had lost fifty pounds.

Staring down at him, at his gaunt, unshaven face, his rotting teeth, the drool running from the side of his open mouth down his cheek, the grime on his forehead, I figured he was down to his last few hundred brain cells. I doubted if he would be of any help.

Was I ever surprised.

Chapter Twenty-one

W hile Janice looked on with obvious distaste, I knelt by the snoring man and shook him awake.

"Huh? What?" His words were slurred. He tried to slap my hand away, but missed. "Go away. G'way."

"Wake up." I shook him again.

He grunted.

"You're not going to wake that one," Janice observed.

"No?" I climbed to my feet and peered into the dumpster. I pulled out a plastic bag and tore it open. I poured the dregs of beer into a single can until it was about a third full. Then I went back to Eric and shook him again. "Hey, Eric. Wake up. I got a beer for you."

That's all it took. He tried unsuccessfully to sit up, so I helped him, then handed him the beer, which he promptly turned up and drained. He spat and puckered his lips. "Hey, there was a cigarette butt in that can."

"Sorry, Eric. I'll get you another. In fact, I'll give you twenty bucks if you'll just answer a few questions."

He blinked several times and tried to focus his bleary eyes on me. "Twenty bucks? Sure. Whatever. Where is it? Let me have it." He stuck out his hand.

I glanced up at Janice who was staring at him in shock. This had been an eye-opening day for her. While those in her stratum of society knew Eric's level existed, they had no concept of the odious reality of that existence. "Not now, not yet, Eric. Answer some questions first."

Hung over and still not fully sober, he became belligerent. "I ain't answering nothing 'til I get the money."

I stood up. "Okay by me. You don't get the money."

He grabbed at my leg with bony fingers. "No, no, I'm sorry. I'm sorry. Don't go. I'll tell you whatever you want."

I squatted. "All right. Ten years ago, you worked with Don Landreth to get Albert Hastings elected governor. Hastings was murdered. You remember that?"

He knit his brows and slowly shook his head as he plowed back though a fuzzy memory soaked with alcohol. "Yeah, yeah, I kinda think so. Now can I have the money?"

"Not yet. A man named Bobby Packard was convicted of the murder, but Don Landreth—you remember Don?"

"Yeah. I couldn't forget Don."

"Don Landreth told me he had proof that would clear Bobby Packard. Do you know what that proof was?"

Eric blinked two or three times. "Is that all you want to know? What proof Don had?"

His question surprised me. I glanced up at Janice whose own face also registered disbelief. "Yeah, yeah. That's all, Eric, that's all."

He closed his eyes and his chin sagged to his chest. I hoped he hadn't passed out again, but moments later, his eyes fluttered open. "Don never told me, but . . . I heard him and Hastings talking once." He squeezed his eyes shut tightly in an effort to concentrate. "Don't remember exactly where it was I heard them talking, but Hastings told Don he wanted to get rid of Sam Bradford."

"The lieutenant governor-elect?"

"Yeah, yeah. Bradford was into drug trafficking big time. Hastings knew if the truth came out, the fallout could ruin him. So . . ." he hesitated, licking his lips as he searched for words. "So, he gave Landreth copies of stuff that proved Bradford was a big time supplier along with some Chink."

"Stuff. Do you mean documents of some sort?"

"Yeah."

"Did you ever see those documents?"

He shook his head drunkenly and dropped his chin to his chest. "No," he looked up sharply, "but that's the truth. That's what I heard. Now can I have the money?" He held out his hand.

A piece was missing from his story. "Not yet. Why would Hastings give Landreth the documents?"

Lavern shrugged. "Backup, I suppose."

"Did you know anything about Bradford's involvement in dealing?"

Once again, he shook his head. "Go ask Don. He'll tell you." His words were slurred.

"I can't, Eric. Landreth's dead."

Lavern blinked, then looked up at me in disbelief.

"They say he committed suicide."

The frail man squeezed his eyes shut. A coarse sob wracked his body and tears dribbled through closed eyes down his bewhiskered cheeks. He looked up at me through pain-wracked eyes. His voice cracked in disbelief. "Don?"

"I'm afraid so."

He looked up at me, trying to focus his eyes. His voice quivering with anguish, he replied, "He wasn't the kind."

I glanced up at Janice. "Kind? What kind?"

"To kill himself."

"Then who do you think did it?"

Moaning softly, he muttered, "Sweet Jesus, sweet Jesus."

I laid my hand on his shoulder. "Eric, listen to me. Who killed him?"

He shook his head slowly. "Don't know."

"Think, Eric, think. Who could have wanted Landreth out of the way?"

Without looking up, he muttered, "It's gotta be Bradford. He's the only one."

"What do you mean, Eric? Why does it have to be Bradford?"

He drew a deep breath and released it slowly, his chest shuddering as he exhaled. "Don warned Hastings that Bradford would never resign. He said Sam Bradford would try to kill Hastings first."

"What did Hastings say?"

Lavern shook his head slowly. "He just laughed."

Janice stared at me in shocked disbelief. I knew why she was so stunned. Not only was Senator Samuel Jefferson Bradford one of her aunt's guests at the Chalk Hills reception the next day, but he was also one of her aunt's closest friends.

"He's doesn't know what he's talking about, Tony. All that alcohol has eaten his brain up." Janice insisted as we headed back to the pickup, skirting the puddles of water in the alley.

"Maybe so, but it's a lead." I hesitated, then added, "And it does fit neatly into a theory that's been wiggling around in the back of my head."

The din and commotion of the bustling city covered the sound of the approaching car until I heard a loud bump and glanced around to see a maroon car hurtling toward us.

At the same moment I spotted the car bearing down on

us I lunged at Janice, knocking her to the ground by the side of a dumpster. In that split second as the car swerved toward us, I tried to catch a glimpse of the driver, and then I hit the ground.

Janice screamed, and in the next instant the car sideswiped the dumpster. I rolled over and looked around for a license number just as the car slid around the corner in a squeal of tires and vanished.

"Are you all right," I said, turning back to Janice, who had managed to sit up.

Eyes wide in disbelief, she stared up at me. "That car almost hit us."

Nodding somberly, I replied. "That was what he had in mind."

"Tony!"

She tried to rise, but I held her down, at the same time gently running my hands over her arms and shoulders. "Take it easy. You sure you're all right? Nothing broken?"

She slowly nodded. "I don't think so." I helped her to her feet, and she gingerly dusted the stains from her brown business suit. "Probably bruised, but—Tony, are you sure? How do you know he tried to hit us?"

Taking her arm, I hurried her to the next street where we took the sidewalk. "You remember the blowout we had on the way back from Huntsville?"

"Yes."

"I can't prove it, but I think someone took a shot the tire."

She frowned. I saw the disbelief in her dark eyes. I then told her about the phone message warning me to stay off the case. "And yesterday," I added, "out on Mopac Expressway, a car sideswiped me, knocked me off the road and down an incline. It was maroon, the same color as this one."

She stared up at me incredulously. "But, why?"

"The only reason I can come up with is that someone wants me—" I hesitated, then said, "wants us—to stop nosing around."

Her eyes grew wide, and her face paled.

On the way to the HEB supermarket near my apartment to pick up the ingredients for the catfish court bouillon I'd promised Beatrice Morrison, I tried to put together a profile of the driver of the maroon car. I had seen him for only a fraction of a second, but I distinctly remembered the black hair, and his stature. He was small. The top of his head barely cleared the steering wheel. I couldn't help remembering the remarks of the witness to my sideswiping the day before. "Looked like a couple Asian guys."

One thing was certain if they were Asian. They sure were the Texan corn-fed variety that Danny O'Banion had talked about out at the County Line Barbecue.

As Janice and I shopped, I bounced my ideas off her. Pushing the empty cart toward the produce section, I began, "First, Lorene Hastings claimed her husband was not jealous of her affair with Bobby Packard, that he knew about it, so perhaps she was right when she claimed Hastings was drunk when he jumped Packard. The bartender supported her allegation. Then Floyd Holloman tells us Red Tompkins had something of value in the heel of his boot. Maybe the videotape. He agreed to sell it to Packard for ten thousand, but when he realized he could get more, he went to that Chinese funeral home. What was the name, Kwockwing? He went inside and dropped out of sight. No one has seen him since."

In the produce section, I picked out choice onions, firm bell peppers, crisp celery, young green onions, and parsley. "How many guests is your aunt expecting?"

"Not many," she shrugged. "The usual hundred or so."

I whistled. "Five gallons of court bouillon won't go far with that many." I headed for the canned goods section. "Next, talked with Sergeant Carpenter who says the slugs taken from Hastings were the same caliber as Packard's Glock. Someone—"

Janice interrupted, a frown on her face. "I've been meaning to ask you. What's a Glock?"

"Huh?" I'd forgotten Janice was a neophyte with firearms. "Oh, a Glock is an automatic made with Polymer Two, a nylon variant that—" I stopped when I saw the frown deepen on her face. "Sorry," I said. "A Glock is a handgun, an automatic."

"Oh."

I picked up some canned tomatoes and tomato paste. "As I was saying, the slugs were lost before the rifling could be tested for a match."

She nodded, but I could tell from the puzzled expression on her face, she wasn't following me. And that was all right. Just voicing my shaky theory so I could hear it was helpful. We moved down the aisle toward the beverage and dairy products.

"Next came Natalie Simms, Hastings' secretary at his real estate office at the time. She heard the shot and moments later saw Packard getting on the elevator, but she had also seen an Asian get off the elevator when she left her desk for the powder room."

We picked up a quart of milk and after some deliberation, a case of Old Milwaukee for my old man.

Janice nodded to the shopping cart. "Is that all?"

"Just about. Catfish and then a visit to frozen foods, and we're finished." I drew a deep breath. "After I left Hastings' ex-secretary I was sideswiped. The cops figured it was accidental. I went along with them more or less, but now—"

She arched an eyebrow, "But now what?"

"One of the witnesses claimed Asians were driving the maroon car that hit me. Today, I only caught a glimpse of the driver of the one who tried to make us part of the asphalt back in the alley. He was small. He could have been Asian. And that ties in neatly with the Asian man Natalie Simms says she saw exit the elevator just before Albert Hastings was murdered," I added.

"What does that mean?"

"That could mean that whoever is trying to tell us to butt out is Asian, and chances are, they're part of the local triad."

Janice shook her head. "Traid? Now, what are you talking about?"

I chuckled. "That's right. I forgot you little rich girls don't learn about Asian gangs in Finishing School."

She slapped at my shoulder. "Don't be so sarcastic. So, what's a triad?"

"An Asian gang. Like the mob in America, the Asians have triads."

"Oh." She nodded her understanding as I picked out five pounds of filleted catfish, then a half dozen frozen dinners. As we waited in the checkout line, I continued. "Next was Pop Wingate. He didn't see the fight between Packard and Hastings, but his shift partner did. He claimed Hastings sucker punched Packard, and then Packard cleaned up the place with Hastings.

"After leaving Wingate, I went to Marble Falls where Don Landreth claimed he had proof Packard was innocent. When I got there, I learned that he had been shot. A bullet in his head."

"Could it have been a suicide?"

I laughed. "Yeah, it could have, but I don't think so. Then came Sally Reston at the day care center. Hastings was a party animal, and Bradford, along with a Chinaman, was at several of the parties. Asians again."

"I remember," Janice said, nodded her head. "And then she told us about Eric Lavern."

"And Lavern claimed Bradford was behind it," I said as I added a couple packs of cigarettes to the purchase and then paid the bill.

"Then the car tried to run us down," Janice put in.

As I loaded the groceries in the back of the Silverado, I said, "Just using drugs as a recreational thing was no big deal. Hastings could always claim like old what's-his-name that he never inhaled. On the other hand, dealing, supplying, trafficking is a big deal."

"So?"

"So, it makes sense that Hastings would want to get rid of Bradford because if Bradford's trafficking came to light, Hastings' political career would head south."

Janice shook her head emphatically as I pulled back onto the Interstate. "I just can't believe Bradford is involved. Have you ever met him? He's a sweet and gentle man."

"Never have," I said, "but I will tomorrow."

She looked around at me in alarm. "Tony! Not at Aunt Beatrice's reception."

"Don't worry." I smiled charmingly at her. "I'll behave."

Chapter Twenty-two

W earing the clothes I'd given him the night before, my old man was squatting on the edge of my small porch, his feet on the sidewalk, bony knees even with his chin. He was smoking a cigarette and drinking the Old Milwaukee he had found in my refrigerator. "Good thing I bought some beer," I said to Janice as we unloaded the groceries.

I gave him a six-pack of cold beer and a pack of cigarettes to keep him on the porch while we put everything away. When we finished Janice patted her stomach. "I don't know about you, but I'm hungry. Do you have anything around here that won't take too long to prepare?"

I winked at her. How about some Cajun caviar, peanut butter and canned figs?"

She laughed, her cheeks dimpling. "With cold milk?"

"With cold milk."

"Tell you what," she said later around her last mouthful of gooey figs and peanut butter. "Why don't you let me help you prepare the court bouillon?"

117

Downing the last of my milk, I replied. "I don't mind the help. You can dice the onions while I make the roux."

"Roux? That's the dark mixture of flour you start it off with, isn't it?"

"I'm surprised you remembered." I reached for a skillet and the cooking oil. "I'll steam the rice in the morning and bring it with me when I pick you up."

The recipe I used had been passed down through generations of Acadians, men as well as women. My *Grandmère* Ola to my Mom, and on to me. *Grandmère* cooked for multitudes, and most of her recipes would feed at least thirty hungry Cajuns. For my use, I had cut the recipe down to serve four or so, which in itself was difficult since there was more to it than just cutting quantities if I wanted to maintain the true flavor.

Now I had to do just the opposite.

The oil in the skillet began to bubble and pop. Time to make the roux.

Roux is the Cajun secret of delicious gumbo, jambalaya, court bouillon, stew, and étouffée. I pulled out the recipe that served four and multiplied the ingredients to make five gallons.

Roux

    8 tablespoons flour
    4 tablespoons vegetable oil
    2 chopped large onions, sautéed
    2 chopped bell peppers

Stir *CONSTANTLY* over medium flame until chocolate-colored. *If it's black, it's burned.*

Add four quarts of water and mix well before adding eight more quarts.

Then for the catfish court bouillon, add:

2 six-ounce cans tomato paste
2 14½ cans whole tomatoes
Bring to boil, stir, then:
Add 1 cup chopped green onion,
1 cup chopped celery,
4 tablespoons chopped parsley.
Reduce heat to medium-low,
simmer thirty minutes.
Add 5 pounds cubed catfish
Salt and pepper to taste.

Simmer for 20 to 30 minutes or until cubed fish
flakes.

"I still don't believe Senator Bradford is involved in all of this, Tony," Janice remarked as we sat at the snack bar, sipping coffee and listening to the sharp little pops of the bubbling court bouillon.

Several years in the PI business had done little to enhance my opinion of human goodness. In fact, it was just the contrary. After a few years dealing with the perversities of human nature, cynicism had set in, and since then, little had surprised me. "You could be right. There's no hard proof, but we'll just have to see how it all plays out."

She arched an eyebrow. "You believe he is involved, don't you?"

Clearing my throat, I replied, "Let me put it this way. Until I know for sure he isn't, then he is."

"Sounds heartless."

I chuckled. "Sometimes that's all there is."

For several moments, she studied me. "We don't have much time left before the . . ." she couldn't say the word.

"I know," I glanced at the calendar, and a sinking feeling began to grow in the pit of my stomach, "we have only three days."

My old man was still squatting on the porch when I left to take Janice back to her condo. Cigarette butts littered the sidewalk, and several empty beer cans lay scattered on the grass. "Back later," I said as we passed.

"It's been nice seeing you, Mr. Boudreaux," Janice said perfunctorily.

With his typical courtesy and eloquence, my old man simply grunted and took another puff off his cigarette.

"How long is he planning to stay?" Janice asked as we drove away.

"No idea," I replied with a shrug. "I'm going to talk to him when I get back to see what he has in mind."

Sarcasm coated her response, "Good luck. Now, what time will you pick me up in the morning?"

"The reception starts at 1 P.M. How about 11:30?"

"In the little car?"

I laughed, "In the little car."

My father was still squatting on the porch when I returned. I'd stopped at a McDonald's on the return trip and picked up some fries and burgers.

I held up the bag. "Hungry? I got us some hamburgers."

"Naw," he looked up at me and gave me a gap-toothed grin. "Ate me some of that there court bouillon." He dragged his tongue over his cracked lips. "Right tasty, boy. You got your Ma's touch."

How I held my temper I'll never know, but I did. With a growl I said, "I made the court bouillon for a party tomorrow. I'll make you some for yourself if you want."

He patted his belly. "Reckon I'm full as a tick. Might tackle the burgers later." His eyes slowly lost their focus and he gazed across the lawn to the cars passing on the street.

I stared at him for another few seconds, then went inside biting my tongue to keep from exploding.

Lifting the lid of the pot of court bouillon, I expected to see the level down several inches, but to my surprise I couldn't tell if he'd eaten any or not. There was a dirty bowl in the sink, so I figured he had. I tossed the bag of burgers on the stove and slid the pot of court bouillon into the refrigerator. Believe it or not, for a couple moments I seriously considered buying a padlock for the refrigerator.

I booted up the computer and to my delight, the information I had requested from Eddie Dyson was in my mailbox. "I don't know how you do it, Eddie," I muttered as I opened his e-mail, "but you're worth every cent."

What I read reinforced my belief that Bobby Packard was innocent. In all his years with A. A. Aggregates and Asphalt, he had never received an unsatisfactory performance report. In fact, most of the reports graded him above average. The last report less than a year before marked him superior, and in the section for comments were the remarks, *Mr. Packard is an outstanding employee who, by his thoroughness and conscientiousness, sets a fine example for his co-workers.*

Those were not the accolades accorded a man fired from his job.

In the last paragraph of his message, Eddie promised me the background checks on Lei Sun Huang and Joey Soong. "And the charge will be higher," he wrote. "Those two are hard to find. Someone has deliberately tried to keep them low-profile."

Quickly, I printed up a hard copy and put it in my files.

At that moment, my old man stumbled in and headed for the refrigerator. I watched him closely, but all he retrieved was a cold beer. He popped the tab and came back into the living room where he plopped down on the couch. "You be going home for Thanksgiving, boy?"

I turned to face him. "Plan on it," I replied flatly, deliberately not elaborating on my plans.

He downed several gulps of beer and dragged his arm over his lips. "Me, I'd like to ride with you if you don't mind."

I didn't answer right away. I studied him, trying to peer behind those wary, animal-like eyes. As much as I hated to admit it, I didn't really like the man. And I didn't really want him in the truck with me for three hundred and ninety miles. "I offered to take you a few years ago. You agreed, and then you took some of my stuff and pawned it. Remember?" I tried to contain my growing irritation with him.

His forehead wrinkled in concentration for a few seconds. He ran bony fingers through his thinning, graying hair. "Can't say I do. You say I hocked some of your stuff?" his thin voice quivered.

"Yeah. A sheep-lined leather coat, VCR, camera—you don't remember?"

He shook his head slowly.

My eyes narrowed. Sarcastically, I began, "You already said you don't remember the family reunion on Whiskey Island last year, so I'm sure you don't remember stea—" I hesitated. Even if it were true, I couldn't say the word, stealing. Instead, I said, "You don't remember selling my laptop computer to a trucker?"

Again, he shook his head. "Sorry, boy. I got no recollection of that neither, but if I did, I'm mighty sorry. It ain't Christian for a father to take from his own son."

He looked so frail and dismayed over the news I almost felt sorry for him, but then I reminded myself that was how he played the game. That's how he had snookered me before. He had me believing he sincerely wanted to change. Then the day before we were to leave for Church Point, he had caught a freight for San Antonio and points west after pocketing three hundred bucks from pawning things he had taken from my apartment.

I tried to keep my voice hard and cold, cutting, "You're right, John. It wasn't Christian, and it wasn't right to take from me. But you did."

His head drooped like a recalcitrant child. "You be right, boy. It was mighty un-Christian-like of me. But, me, I've changed. I seen the light."

Shaking my head in frustration, I replied, "Come on now, John. You've told me that before. Why should I believe it now?"

He looked up, his eyes sad and begging. "Boy, This time, I mean it. Me, I want to change. I ain't long for this world. I'd sure like to make everything right with my family."

My eyes narrowed as I stared at him. I clenched my teeth. He was lying. I knew he was lying, but I felt my resolve slipping. I still didn't like him, but he was my father.

What was I to do? As soon as I asked myself the question, I knew. I shook my head in disgust at how my emotions had suddenly taken over my good sense. "All right, John. If you want to ride over to Church Point with me, you can."

And who knows? I told myself as emotions overrode common sense. *Maybe he does mean it this time.*

Chapter Twenty-three

Next morning at 5:00, I rolled out of bed and staggered into the kitchen to put on the coffee. My eyes half-closed, I stumbled past my old man on the couch and stopped at the aquarium to feed Oscar. My hand froze when I started to shake the small container.

Oscar was floating belly up.

I stared at him for several moments before I realized he was dead. I touched his belly. He bobbed down, then back up. "Poor little guy," I muttered. Still, he had lived longer than he was supposed to, even after surviving Jack's chemical attack.

Instead of conducting his funeral in the bathroom, I took him outside and buried him in the flowerbed. He had made me a comforting little companion after my divorce and deserved better than the toilet.

I checked the thermometer. Fifty degrees. The sky was clear. The day would warm quickly.

By 10:00 A.M., the temperature had hit the low seventies, a magnificent day for a drive in the Model T.

I placed the rice and court bouillon on the floorboard on the passenger's side. "I'll be back in two or three

124

hours," I told my old man. The one positive aspect to his being here was that I had a perfect excuse to leave the party early—but not until I had visited with Samuel Bradford, senior Senator from the state of Texas. And as I promised Janice, I would behave myself.

The Model T was both fun and a challenge to drive—fun because of the attention it drew, and a challenge because of the coordination demanded by two forward speeds and a reverse initiated by the use of foot pedals. At times my feet were dancing like the proverbial cat on a hot tin roof.

Another small challenge was the fact the little car did not respond to commands instantaneously, like modern automobiles. There is more play in the steering, so the car actually turns a few moments after the wooden steering wheel is moved. It's quirky, but a driver adjusts, which I finally managed to do after running over the curb several times turning into Janice's driveway.

Now, as we tooled along Loop 360 at a steady thirty miles an hour in the outside lane, I continued to check the mirror for a maroon car, trying to appear casual so as not to alarm Janice. I spotted three or four, and each time I turned into a bundle of nerves until the car passed.

I frowned when I spotted a Cadillac convertible weaving through the traffic and changing lanes as it rapidly drew closer. It pulled up beside us and honked. We looked around into the grinning faces of Diane and Jack. They both waved, and we waved back. Jack yelled, but the wind blew his words away. I shrugged and shook my head.

He waved again, and they sped away.

"Well, she certainly didn't lose any time," Janice snapped.

"Uh, oh. Someone's claws are showing." I glanced at her.

She shot me a blistering look, then smiled. "I guess that was a little too catty."

"Looks like the two of them hit it off."

"At least, she isn't hanging around you."

I suppressed a grin. "Yeah, that's okay. But you know, it is tough on a guy's ego to be dropped like that."

She looked around at me in disbelief, trying to figure out if I was serious or not. When she saw the grin slide onto my lips, she slapped playfully at my arm. "You have enough of an ego as it is."

Beatrice Morrison's receptions were the talk of Austin society. Everyone who was anyone or who thought he was anyone went to any length to wheedle, wangle, or finagle an invitation.

True to her word, Beatrice's caterers dumped my court bouillon and steamed rice into silver serving bowls. God forbid simple aluminum pots touch her blue Provençal table motifs—tablecloths to rednecks like me.

Around 12:00 NOON, guests started arriving, and by 1:00 P.M., a chattering crowd milled beneath the blue and white marquis that was half the size of a football field. The tent stood in the middle of a grassy quadrangle surrounded by a neatly-trimmed, ten-foot Privet Hedge. An eight-foot semi-circular arch had been cut in each side of the hedge, allowing access and egress.

A string quartet played Beethoven and Debussy at one end of the tent while a large bar did landslide business at the other. Cynicism insisted there was a direct correlation between various musical selections and the amount of traffic at the bar at certain times.

As at every other one of these functions that we had attended, Janice left me to my own devices while she remained at her aunt's side. In B.A.A.—that's Before Alcoholics Anonymous—I had occupied my idle time at these receptions by seeing how big a dent I could put in Aunt Beatrice's booze supply. Since then, I simply passed the time wandering through the crowd, sipping soda and lime and people-watching.

I found an empty table near the musicians and settled in for a sampling of Austin's upper-class culture.

Beethoven and Debussy are recognized as classical music geniuses. No reflection on their brilliance, but I can't tell "Moonlight Sonata" from "Clair de Lune." To me, their plaintive strains could never compete with my deep appreciation of the Cajun beat of Fernest Arceneaux's rendition of "Jolie Blonde," or Waylon Thibodeaux's "Perrodin Two-Step."

When the dark limo pulled into the parking lot beyond the privet hedge, I was on my second club soda, which I might point out does nothing to enhance my appreciation of classical music the way a half dozen bourbons "neat" once did. A hulking figure emerged from the driver's side and stared over the top of the car at the milling crowd.

There was only one person in Texas that size. Godzilla, aka. Huey, Danny O'Banion's bodyguard, driver, and designated hit man. And it didn't take any musical genius to tell me why they were here. Taking one last sip from my glass, I set it down on the fancy blue tablecloth and headed across freshly mown lawn to the parking lot.

I spotted Senator Bradford mixing in the crowd. I glanced at the limo, then back to Bradford. He could wait.

The back door opened as I drew near. I paused before climbing in and grinned up at Huey who stared impassively at me through the slits that hid his eyes. "Hey there, Huey. Pull off anybody's arm today?"

He said nothing as I slipped into the limo. Huey closed the front door but remained outside, giving Danny and me our privacy.

"He's going to pull off yours one of these days if you

irritate him too much, Tony." A crooked grin slid over Danny's face. "So, how's the job going?"

One thing about Danny. He had never believed in wasting time.

I answered seriously, "It's going. In the last four days, I've talked to several people, most of whom figure Hastings got what he deserved." I went into detail about what I had learned, but with each detail, the furrows on his forehead deepened. I related the warning phone call, the sideswiping incident, the attempted rundown, and the death of Don Landreth.

When I finished, he stared at me for several seconds, then said. "I don't hear a thing that we can use for Bobby."

"I agree, but we're getting closer. Tomorrow, I'm making a trip to the County Clerk's office downtown."

"What's at the County Clerk's office?"

"I'm not sure. I want to look up some businesses to find out who owns them. There might be something there."

"I don't understand, Tony. Seems like that's a waste of time, just like being out here today instead of working." His eyes grew cold and his normally fair skin reddened. "This is the second of the month. Bobby rides the needle on the fourth," he said impatiently.

"Everything points to Sen. Sam Bradford's involvement." I glanced back at the reception. "I saw him a moment ago. I'm going to visit with him here. If we can establish a connection between him and the triad and their drugs, then maybe we have a chance."

My explanation seemed to somewhat mollify Danny's impatience. He lowered his voice, "What about that information I gave you?"

I glanced at the empty driver's seat. "I'm expecting something this afternoon. I'll act on it as soon as possible."

"You need to work fast, Tony." I read the veiled warning in his words.

"You know me, Danny," I replied, eyeing him coldly, "I don't lie. I'm doing the best I can. This case is cold, ten years cold."

He studied me skeptically. "I'm getting worried, Tony. Big time."

I grunted, "You think I'm not?"

Back at the reception, I picked up another soda with a slice of lime and wandered among the guests, searching for Bradford, hoping to buttonhole him for a few moments.

I had seen him earlier, but now he was nowhere to be found. I hoped he hadn't left.

Taking a seat at an empty table near the bar, I absently studied the guests while I pondered the last few days, searching for a link, or any connection that would confirm my suspicions about the senator. I had toyed with the idea that Landreth's death was part of the grand scheme, whatever that scheme might be. I truly believed that someone killed Landreth so he wouldn't give me the proof to clear Packard. If that were true, then that someone must have overheard or intercepted Landreth's message to me.

Without warning, a guttural voice broke into my musings. "Mind if I join you, Boudreaux?"

I looked up into the impassive face of Huey's double, Godzilla II.

Before I could answer, another voice rumbled to my right. "Me too." This Neanderthal was only about three-quarters the size of the first. He was puny, probably not much over two hundred and fifty pounds. His chin looked as if it had been sculpted from granite, and in the middle of it, there was a cleft deep enough to hold a quarter. Both men looked out of place in the expensive suits they wore.

I was in no position to refuse. "Be by guests, boys." My brain raced, wondering what they had in mind. Surely they wouldn't waste me in the middle of Beatrice Morrison's annual reception. Not even Joe Basco, the mob boss in New Orleans, would risk her wrath by causing chaos during one of her precious events.

Cleft Chin leaned forward. His voice had the texture of gravel. "We know you was hired to do a job. Nobody can blame you for trying to make a buck. My boss is concerned that if you keep nosing around, you might not have the chance to spend the buck."

He couldn't have made his point any plainer.

I cut my eyes to his cohort, who sat motionless, his black eyes piercing me with a look that left no question in my mind that he would not hesitate to carry out that promise with great delight. I wanted to tell them what they could do with their concern, but my one hundred and sixty-five pounds against their five or six hundred-plus seemed insane odds, even to a dummy like me. Nodding slowly, I replied, "I appreciate your boss' concern for my health."

They stared coldly at me for a few seconds longer, then without another word, rose and disappeared into the crowd of guests.

I made my way after them through the laughing, guests but jerked to a halt when I spotted the two goons crossing the parking lot. I quickly stepped back a few feet into the crowd, knowing I could see them easily enough, but they would have trouble picking out one individual deep in the crowd.

As I watched through one of the arches in the hedge, they halted when a white stretch limo pulled up to them. A window hissed down. Cleft Chin leaned forward, apparently speaking with someone in the stretch.

He shook his head, stepped back, turned, and stared

back at the tent. I moved behind a portly gentleman and peered around him. Cleft Chin turned back to the limo, and shook his head again. The window hissed up as the limo pulled away, heading for the exit that was beyond the hedge on the far side of the tent. I quickly wound my way between clusters of guests, hoping to reach the other side before the limo disappeared.

Pausing, I glanced around to see if anyone was watching, and then casually wandered across the manicured lawn to the opening in the hedge just as the limo braked at the exit, turned left, and headed for the highway.

I read the license plate, then hastily repeated the combination of characters while I fumbled for a scrap of paper on which to jot the number, *LSH-YOT*. Another job for me at the courthouse next morning.

Mingling once again, I searched for Bradford, but he was nowhere to be seen. I'd missed him but I eased my disappointment by telling myself I'd try his local office in the morning.

We didn't leave until after 4:00 P.M., later than I had expected. Aunt Beatrice was effusive in her thanks for the court bouillon and insisted that Cajun cuisine would be part of her annual reception in the future.

Janice was ecstatic over the success of the reception and kept up a steady stream of observations about the party. I was paying more attention to her than the traffic and didn't see the Peterbilt semi barrelling toward us as we putt-putted along Loop 360 at a vulnerable thirty miles per hour.

Chapter Twenty-four

"I had a wonderful time," Janice gushed, glancing up at me. "Aunt Beatrice was extremely pleased with the—" the smile on her face froze, then exploded into wide-eyed terror. "Tony!"

I jerked around to see a tire the size of a small house staring me in the face. I yanked the wheel to the right. It seemed like an hour before the Runabout responded, finally bouncing over the concrete shoulder.

The Peterbilt tractor, *sans* trailer, followed.

I headed across the grass, steering toward the access road. I crossed my fingers that something wouldn't break when we jumped off the curb down a few inches to the concrete.

The snarling grill of the roaring tractor was right behind us.

Luckily we hit a gap in the traffic and shot across the access road into the empty parking lot of a deserted warehouse; unluckily, the Peterbilt hit the same gap.

A dozen or so security light posts in the parking lot were mounted on concrete pedestals two feet or so in diameter, and about two or three feet high. Just as I passed one, I whipped the Runabout to the left. Our only advantage was that we could turn in a smaller radius than the semi.

Janice clutched the dashboard, her eyes fixed on the towering black Peterbilt as it careened in a circle and bore down on us. "Tony! What are we going to do?"

For once, I didn't have a wisecrack. My feet tap-danced on the pedals. "Stay away from him. At least until someone sees us playing tag and calls the cops." I can't say we raced along the side of the parking lot. Putt-putted is more like it, but we managed to swing around another pedestal as the roaring tractor howled past.

Desperation pounded in my chest. I clenched my fingers around the steering wheel feeling like a three-legged mouse dodging the cat from Hades in a locked closet.

For the third time, I whipped around a pedestal, and the Peterbilt roared past, missing my back bumper by inches. An eighteen-wheeler tractor without a trailer is fast, and I couldn't afford to take any chances. I cast a hasty glance at the access road, praying for the flashing lights and the wail of a police cruiser. But no one seemed to be paying us any attention. Where were the cops when you needed them?

I shot a look over my left shoulder in time to see the black tractor with the snarling chrome grill whip into a circle, the rear wheels bouncing up and down as they slid sideways. I lined up a pedestal between the tractor and us, stopping far enough from it so I could dart (I use that word loosely) either left or right depending on which side of the pedestal the Peterbilt swerved.

Engine screaming, the massive black cab with the snarling grill headed straight for us. Swallowing the lump in my throat, I waited, watching for the slightest hint of which way he would turn. "Come on," I muttered, "Turn, turn!"

Janice grabbed my arm. "Tony? It—It looks like—" her words stuck in her throat. And then she screamed.

The Peterbilt slammed into the pedestal. For a moment, everything stood still, and then the thirty-foot light pole flipped over the back of the tractor, which veered to our left from the impact. I headed to our right.

I spotted a sidewalk that cut behind a chain link fence at the far corner of the parking lot. Out of desperation, I headed for it, crossing my fingers that the narrow ribbon of concrete led somewhere. When I reached it, I saw that a drainage ditch paralleled it on the left so I cut between the chain link fence and the ditch.

The Peterbilt decided to take a shortcut. He angled toward me, ignoring the fence. I kicked the Runabout up to its top speed, which was slightly faster than a kiddy car powered by foot pedals, but I quickly realized I couldn't dodge the angle taken by the Peterbilt.

I slammed on the brakes and in the midst of a grinding and gnashing of gears, slammed the little car into reverse.

The lumbering truck hit the fence, ripping a section of the galvanized netting from the ground. The fence tangled under the truck's front wheels, jamming the steering. In the next seconds, the truck swept in front of us dragging fifty feet of chain link in its wake and plunged into the concrete drainage ditch, coming to an abrupt halt with its rear wheels spinning in the air.

We shot forward and bounced off the sidewalk onto the street. I threw a quick glance back at the tractor and spotted a figure sprinting across the parking lot toward the freeway.

While he was too distant for me to discern his features, he was tall and bulky and sported a prominent beer belly. He was definitely not Asian.

We were both shaken.

Janice remained silent for the first few blocks. Finally,

she looked up at me, her face almost as pale as mine. "That truck was trying to kill us, wasn't it?"

I turned down the street to her condo. "I think you'd better not come with me anymore. Somebody out there is getting serious."

She studied me, her eyes reflecting hurt and disappointment. "You think I'm just a silly little rich girl, don't you, Tony? You don't think I can take it when things get tough, do you?"

I kept my eyes on the road ahead and the road behind. "I think that what you want to believe doesn't reflect the truth of the job. It can be dangerous. You just had a taste of that. I don't want you hurt."

We pulled up in front of her condo. I walked her to the door and she looked at me hopefully. "Do you want to come in?"

"Thanks, but I got my old man back at my place—if I have any place left," I added with a grin.

She smiled weakly. "See you later then."

I leaned down and touched my lips to hers.

Back in my apartment, I found my old man sleeping on the couch. I looked around. No furniture was missing; the computer was on the desk; appliances still in the kitchen; even the toilet bowl remained in place.

Luck had smiled upon me. Maybe John Roney *was* trying to set things right.

I glanced at the empty aquarium and grimaced. It was going to seem odd without Oscar around. With a shrug, I plopped down in front of the computer to update my notes and plan for the next day.

While I had blown the opportunity to interview Senator Bradford, I did have the personalized license number of the white stretch, the owner of which, in all probability, initiated the fourth attempt to either frighten me off or kill me—five attempts total if I counted the two goons at the reception.

I made a note to look up the owner of license number LSH-YOT and the legal descriptions of A. A. Aggregates and Asphalt as well as that of the Kwockwing Funeral Home.

Glancing back over my cards, I paused at Eric Lavern's assertion that Bradford was behind the entire scheme. I started thinking about Don Landreth. He had been murdered while waiting for me. The next logical question was did someone murder him because of me, because of my investigation? I believed so, but I had no proof.

I leaned back in my chair, balancing it on the two back legs, and muttered, "If they got to him because of what he was going to give me, how did they find out about it?"

There was only one explanation. Someone must have tapped his phone line. Nodding slowly, I realized there was only one way I could be sure. And if the line was tapped, the logical conclusion had to be that whoever had murdered Landreth and made the attempts on my life would stop at nothing to prevent a stay of Bobby Packard's execution.

Once Packard was executed, the identity of the real killers would be forever hidden.

Thinking back to my visit with Danny O'Banion when he pointed out there was very little substance to what I had uncovered in the last three days, I had to agree. But now I had a chance to come up with something solid. While the proof might not be irrefutable, it would be enough to suggest that Bobby Packard had been framed.

And how could I prove some sort of conspiracy? By determining if Landreth's phone line was tapped.

* * *

My old man was still sleeping. I checked the refrigerator. One six-pack left. I shrugged. *Not bad. Only eighteen beers in twenty-four hours. Hey, that was less than one an hour.* I slipped on my windbreaker.

"Six-fifteen," I mumbled glancing at my watch. That would put me in Marble Falls around 7:30. I didn't figure I'd have trouble finding Landreth's place. The rancher in the convenience store had said it was five or six miles out on Farm Road 301. That had to be a rural mail route, which meant there would be a mailbox at the side of the road.

Just as I closed the door behind me, Janice's Miata pulled into my drive.

"Hi," she said brightly, climbing out of the little roadster. "Are you going somewhere?" She eyed my windbreaker.

"Marble Falls," I said.

She didn't reply for several seconds, expecting me to elaborate. When I didn't, she asked, "For Packard?"

"Yeah." I changed the subject, hoping she would go back to her place, "What are you up to?"

"Oh, nothing," she shrugged. "I was just wondering how you were after this afternoon."

I couldn't help chuckling. She was worrying about me when I was the one worrying about her. "No problem. It's all part of the job. How about you?"

She nodded, "Tony?"

"Yeah?"

The glow from the porch light cast her face in shadowy relief. "May I go with you?" she chewed on her bottom lip.

"You'll be bored sick."

"I don't care. You know, I was very serious when I said I wanted to help you, to be a part of what you do."

For a moment, I started to refuse, but I didn't want to hurt her feelings. Besides, she could stay in the pickup while I slipped past the crime scene ribbons and into the house. "Like I said, it'll be boring. Just a ride out to Marble Falls and back."

"That's okay with me. What's out there?"

"I want to check the telephone to see if the line was tapped."

"Tapped? How do you do that?"

I gestured to her Miata. "If you'll move your car so I can get out I'll explain on the way."

While she moved her small car, I fumbled through my toolbox of security gadgets and pulled out a pocket-sized TTD system designed to recognize taps. I dropped it into my pocket.

Chapter Twenty-five

Out on Farm Road 301 far away from the lights of Marble Falls, the stars filled the night with a bluish glow. Beginning at mile four, we slowed at each mailbox until we found Landreth's. Lined by scrub oaks, the drive curved between two small hills within a hundred yards of the fence. I stayed on the farm road.

Janice frowned, "Why didn't you stop?"

"In case someone was watching."

Her eyes widened. " 'Watching!' Who would be watching?"

"Anyone," I muttered as we rounded a curve and pulled up behind a small rise. I flipped off the headlights, turned the pickup around and parked on the shoulder of the road.

"Anyone? Sounds paranoid to me," she replied, teasing.

I squinted into the night. "The more schizo-paranoid you are in this business, sweetheart, the longer you'll live," I said in my best Humphrey Bogart imitation as I opened the door. "I'm going to cut across the pasture to the drive. You wait."

"But, what about you? How will I know if you're all right?"

139

"Don't worry about me. Just you stay put."

"Tony please," her tone pleaded with me.

I wished I had insisted she stay at home. I had work to do, and I didn't need any distractions. But she was there. "All right. You have your cell phone?"

"Yes," she patted her purse, "in here."

"I'll keep you posted. But whatever you do, Janice, don't call me. Okay?"

"Okay."

With the tap-defeat bug in my pocket and a small flashlight in my hand, I hurried across the pasture of wiry grass and rock to Landreth's drive, then scurried through the shadows of the scrub oaks along the asphalt road. Just beyond the two hills lay the ranch, with a main house and several outbuildings. The windows were dark and ominous. I knelt behind an oak and warily studied the buildings.

The crime scene ribbon fluttered briefly in a light breeze. I crouched and crept forward, pausing every few seconds. From the hill behind me, I heard a night bird call, and beyond the dark silhouette of the main house, an owl hooted.

When I reached the small hedge around the lawn I paused, straining for any telling sound. I heard nothing out of the ordinary. On the balls of my feet, I hurried to the front door and pressed back into the shadow of the porch.

My heart thudded in my chest. I waited, listening.

Nothing.

Slowly, I turned the knob. The door opened. I paused once again, peering into the complete blackness of the room. The house had a musty smell with a trace of stale cigarette smoke.

In one quick move, I slipped inside and pressed up

against the wall by the doorjamb. After a moment, I flipped on my small flashlight, keeping the beam on the floor to prevent any glow being seen through the windows from outside.

I didn't know what kind of tap might have been used. If there was a single line into the house, any phone jack would reveal the tap. But if there were multiple lines, I might have to check every phone in the house, a time-consuming job, with every second increasing my risk of exposure.

I played the thin light beam along the wall about a foot off the floor, searching for a jack. There was none in the foyer. The next room was the living room. I discovered a jack.

Quickly, I unplugged the phone and inserted the line into the TTD. Nothing happened.

Muttering a soft curse, I realized that since there was no line tap here, the probability of multiple lines increased, and that meant I had to check each receiver in the house.

I was heading for the next room, cursing under my breath when a thought stopped me in my tracks. *What if they had already removed the tap? I could be wasting valuable time.* But I had no choice. Taking a deep breath, I continued the search for phone jacks.

Each room had a receiver, I discovered but I went through the entire house without any luck. The last room was the sunroom, simply an enclosed back porch. I paused, shining the tiny beam on my watch. Almost 8:30. I'd been inside forty-five minutes. Too long—much too long.

I found the jack and traced the line to a small table beside a chaise lounge. Anxious to get out of the house, I disconnected the line, plugged it into the TTD. My heart jumped into my throat as a red light flashed on the TTD.

This was it. This must have been the receiver Landreth used to return my call. Someone had indeed tapped it, which reinforced my theory that Landreth had been murdered because he claimed to have the proof to free Bobby Packard.

Quickly, I unplugged the TTD, dropped it back into my pocket, and slipped out the back door. I leaped from the porch and paused at the corner of the house to punch in Janice's cell number. Just as it rang, a dark figure stepped from around the corner and faced me. "Hold it right there, buddy, or you're dead meat."

I froze, squinting into the darkness in an effort to discern his features.

"Okay turn around and put your hands behind you."

I felt the light bulk of the TTD in my pocket and the cell phone in my hand. Maybe, if I threw them at him and leaped aside at the same time, I might have a chance.

But before I could even flinch, the cold muzzle of a handgun poked the back of my neck. A guttural voice said, "He said put your hands behind you."

Dropping the cell phone to the ground at my feet, I did as he said, figuring if they were going to send me wherever they had sent Landreth, they would already have put some holes in me. "All right, boys. Here they are," I said as I moved my hands behind my back.

One of them used a plastic tie to cinch my wrists together. The narrow band cut into my flesh.

"Easy," I shouted, hoping Janice could hear what was going on, "you're cutting off the blood."

"Tough," he growled, giving me a shove and sending me stumbling across the lawn. "All right, head for the barn."

The other one, the one with the guttural voice, laughed. "When they find you in the barn, they'll figure you hung yourself because you killed Landreth."

My blood ran cold. Their concept was as ludicrous as their intent. "That'll cut no ice, boys," I said desperately. "You think anyone would believe that I was so filled with remorse that I'd come back out two days later and hang myself? What'd you do, see that plot on 'movie of the week?'"

"Shut up, you," one growled, slamming me in the back with his gun.

I staggered forward, grimacing at the sharp pain.

"Cut it out, Mick. We don't want no bruises on him."

Mick grumbled, "Just tell him to shut his trap."

"Don't worry. It'll be shut soon enough."

I knew then my only chance was to make a break. I'd rather be shot down trying to escape than left dangling from a rope inside the barn.

We were within twenty yards of the barn when a white pickup with its headlights off roared around the corner of the barn and headed directly for the two goons behind me.

Janice!

The two button men shouted and fired at the pickup bearing down on them but at the last moment, they leaped aside. I took off running while Janice whipped the Silverado around and headed back at the two men stumbling to their feet.

"Yaaa," one yelled as he again threw himself aside. The other tried to stand his ground. He managed to squeeze off one shot, but at the last moment, decided discretion was the better part of valor and leaped from the path of the truck.

Janice slowed as she caught up with me. "Tony! Jump in the back."

I didn't argue. I leaped in head first, twisting onto my shoulder as I slammed onto the bed of the pickup. "Go, go, go," I yelled. But then I felt the Silverado whipping around for another pass at the two goons. "No, no, no," I yelled, but at seventy miles an hour, my words were blown away by the wind.

There were two small pops, and then nothing. To my relief, we kept going straight. When we reached Farm Road, Janice slammed on the brakes and jumped in the back, to try to free me.

"Hurry. They might be coming after us right now."

Her fingers fumbled. "I can't get it open."

"My pocket. Get my knife."

Her fingers flew. She muttered an unladylike curse. "I broke a fingernail opening this thing," she muttered, quickly slicing the plastic tie.

"I'll buy you new ones," I said, helping her from the pickup bed into the truck. "Let's get going while we can."

Seconds later, we were driving toward Marble Falls and on to Austin.

"That was a nifty bit of driving," I said, keeping my eyes on both the road ahead and the traffic behind.

She looked up at me. "It wasn't bad, was it?"

"How'd you know what was going on?" I glanced at her, puzzled.

"I saw them drive in but I didn't know what was going on until I heard everything on the cell phone."

All I could do was shake my head.

The oncoming headlights lit up the big grin on her face. "Now, aren't you glad you brought me tonight?"

I shook my head. "Absolutely. You saved my bacon back there. Whoever those goons were, they were going to make me the fall guy for Landreth's death."

She frowned. "I don't understand what good that would do."

"It would solve a murder and get me out of the way."

For several seconds, Janice remained silent. I knew she was agonizing over someone in particular but decided to keep quiet unless she asked.

Chapter Twenty-six

By the time I followed Janice back to her condo and returned to my apartment, it was almost midnight. My place was still dark as it had been when we picked up her Miata. I figured my old man must be sleeping. We were out of Old Milwaukee, I guessed.

I should have known better. He wasn't sleeping. He had vanished.

This was no big surprise, I told myself as I searched through the apartment to see if he'd carried off anything. The garage door was still locked, so I assumed everything in there must be intact.

Stepping back onto the porch, I peered up and down the street in a futile effort to spot him and finally shook my head. There was no telling where he was; no telling when I'd see him again; no telling what he had in mind. And to my surprise, I felt a tinge of disappointment. Without being aware of it, I had begun to hope.

With a sigh, I went back inside. I had a busy day ahead.

It turned out to be busier than I had thought. At 4:00 A.M. the phone rang.

145

Groggy from too little sleep, I fumbled for the receiver. "Yeah," I managed to mutter.

"Tony?"

There was a familiar ring to the voice, but I was too sleepy to make the effort to pinpoint it. "Huh?"

"This is Joe Ray Burrus."

Instantly, I became alert. Joe Ray worked the Evidence Room down at Austin P.D. and he was always a reliable source. He and I had gone through the first three years at U. T. before he transferred to Sam Houston University and changed his major to criminal justice.

Joe Ray was one of those free-thinking rebels who preferred remaining just within the bounds of convention for the sake of comfort, the comfort of a steady paycheck. From time to time, depending upon how a proposition struck him, he pushed the envelope, on occasion kicking a hole in it.

If he was calling me at this time of morning, it had to be important. "Hey. What's wrong? Do you need something?"

"Naw, I'm fine. I'm working the vampire shift for Joe Simmons." He paused a moment. "Reason I'm calling is that a guy with the same last name as yours was tossed in the drunk tank. *Boudreaux*. There ain't too many of them Boudreaux-type folks around here in Austin."

Rolling my eyes, I replied, "His name wouldn't happen to be John Roney would it?"

He chuckled, "Sounds familiar, huh?"

"Yeah," I muttered a couple choice expletives, "it's my old man. He was staying out here with me, but when I got in earlier, he was gone. Truth is, I was kind of hoping he'd grabbed a freight for San Antonio and points west." Strangely enough, as soon as I made the sarcastic quip, I felt guilty.

Joe Ray laughed. "Sorry to disappoint you. I don't know where they found him, but he's here. You can get him out in the morning."

Needless to say, sleep was out of the question. I plopped down in front of my computer and booted it up.

In checking my mail, I spotted a file from Eddie Dyson and quickly opened it.

The file contained the background checks I had requested on Lei Sun Huang, whom Danny O'Banion claimed headed up the Ying On triad, and Joey Soong, the top man in the Sing Leon tong, along with a personal note from Eddie.

Scanning the pitifully thin file, I saw that both were born in America in the sixties and Joey Soong ran a small laundry while Lei Sun Huang had an interest in the Kwockwing Funeral Home.

That was all.

I read Eddie's note.

Sorry, Tony. There was nothing on these two except Social Security numbers. They don't even have drivers' licenses. It's like they were just born. No charge for this one, pal.

I reread the file. The only thing I recognized was the Kwockwing Funeral Home, the one into which Red Tompkins had disappeared ten years earlier.

Pulling out my note cards, I studied the plans I had made for the morning. I wanted to look up the owner of license number LSH-YOT and the owners of A. A. Aggregates and Asphalt as well as that of the Kwockwing Funeral Home and now of Joey Soong's laundry. To find information on the three businesses, I had to have legal descriptions. From the legal descriptions, I could get owners' names.

Pulling out the telephone directory, I copied the addresses.

The Travis County Courthouse opened at 8:00. My first stop would be the tax office where, with the addresses, I could obtain a legal description, with which the County Clerk's office could then look up names of owners.

I wasn't really sure just what I was looking for, but I knew I was closing in on it. The attempts on my life were proof enough. The logical extension of my thinking was that someone wanted Packard dead. Looking back over the last couple days, that someone had to have a broad sphere of influence—like Sen. Samuel Jefferson Bradford would have.

Thirty minutes before the courthouse opened, I pulled into a slot in the parking lot behind the police station. For several moments I studied the station house. I'm ashamed to admit it, but I was seriously considering letting my old man sweat it out in the drunk tank while I tackled the last couple days of saving Bobby Packard.

The date was November 3.

If I failed, then at 6:00 P.M. the next day, November 4, sodium thiopental, the first of the three chemicals used to carry out the death penalty, would be injected into Bobby Packard's arm to anaesthetize him. One minute later, pancuronium bromide would flood his system to relax muscles, collapsing the diaphragm and lungs, followed sixty seconds later with potassium chloride to stop the heart.

Within seven minutes, the execution would be over. And all for the frugal cost to the Texas taxpayers of $86.08.

I told myself I didn't have time to keep up with my old man. *Use some common sense, Tony*, I told myself. *Let*

him sit in jail. At least, he can't get into trouble there. Get
him out later.

All logical, sensible thoughts of course, but surprisingly,
I found myself marching across the parking lot into the station house. I couldn't silence the little voice in the back of
my head that kept saying, *Maybe this time. Maybe this time.*

By 9:30, John Roney and I were back at the truck. I was
a couple hundred dollars poorer, and we had a court date
in four weeks. Mentally, I kissed the two hundred bucks
good-bye knowing full well he'd never make the court
date, but at least, my old man was out of jail.

"Climb in," I said, "and wait for me." I pointed to the
courthouse. "I have a couple errands to run. I'll be right
back."

I visited the tax office first where I found the legal
description of all three properties. My next stop was the
County Clerk's office where I requested the name of the
owner of the limo with the license number LSH-YOT as
well as the three businesses. "I might be interested in pur-
chasing one of them," I told the young clerk.

Sitting on a bench in the hall outside of the County
Clerk's office ten minutes later, I stared at the documents
in my hands, unable to believe what I had discovered.

Both A. A. Aggregates and Kwockwing Funeral Home
were incorporated, and Samuel Jefferson Bradford served
on the board of each one. I pondered the information.
Bradford on the board of A. A. Aggregates and Kwockwing
Funeral home could explain the appearance of the Peterbilt
tractor that tried to turn the Model T into junk, and the
Asians that did their best to do the same to Janice and me
in the alley.

I continued reading.

The president of Kwockwing Funeral Home Incorporated was none other than Lei Sun Huang, the same Lei Sun Huang who was the alleged leader of the Ying On triad.

I looked at the name of the owner of the limo. Again, Lei Sun Huang. "Why didn't you see that, dummy," I muttered, observing the license number. LSH-YOT. Lei Sun Huang of the Ying On triad. I shook my head at their audacity. "They even have their own personalized plates," I muttered.

There were several Asians listed as officers of the Kwockwing corporation. On impulse, I jotted the names of the five officers and headed back to the County Clerk's office.

I went to the DBA line. DBA meant *doing business as,* and all prospective business owners, *doing business as,* must register their names and the names of their business with the respective county.

I handed the older clerk a list of names and requested the name of their businesses.

Quickly, she entered the request into a computer, and within moments, the printer spit out the information. She handed me the reports. "Only two came up, sir. That'll be ten dollars."

Back out in the hall, I scanned the reports. Chang Yulan owned a medium-sized service business on the east side of Austin, the Seven Seas Import-Export.

The second name, Lao Ning, ran a chain of carwashes, inscrutably named Bobby's Carwash.

For several moments, I stood motionless, contemplating the information before me. Senator Bradford's position as board member of both Kwockwing Funeral Home Incorporated and A. A. Aggregates and Asphalt

Incorporated firmly convinced me that he was part of the efforts to scare me away from the case.

Now, I had to come up with the hard proof. I glanced at my watch and whistled softly. Whatever I did, I had to do it fast.

I hesitated as I approached my pickup. The front seat was empty. The old man had vanished again. I shook my head and cursed. *I should have known better. So much for maybes.*

I slid behind the wheel. I knew very little about Asian culture, and I didn't have time to learn its nuances now. I would just have to keep doing what I did best—blunder ahead. I crossed my fingers that Joe Ray Burrus's assertion that the Song Leon tong and the Ying On triad hated each other. Otherwise, I could be walking into something that I couldn't get out of just like Red Tompkins did when he walked into the Kwockwing Funeral Home.

I decided to provide myself some insurance. I called Joe Ray Burrus. "You know where the Soong Laundry is located?"

"Sure. It's on Seventy-eighth Street near Huston Tillotson College. Joey Soong runs it. What's up?"

"Do me a favor. I'm going out there to talk to him. If you don't hear from me in an hour, send a car out there."

He grew serious. "You all right, Tony? What are you up to?"

"I don't know. I just don't want to disappear like Red Tompkins did."

"Red who?"

"I'll explain later. Just help me out on this, okay?"

"Okay. One hour."

Chapter Twenty-seven

My first surprise came when I pulled up in front of Soong Laundry. Instead of a tiny hovel squeezed between two clapboard buildings in the manner portrayed by the old westerns, it was a well-kept building of white brick and glass surrounded on three sides by a professionally-maintained landscape. In the rear parking lot sat a half dozen sparkling-white delivery trucks.

The second surprise was the smiling young lady who greeted me when I entered. I guess I was expecting barely intelligible singsong speech, but instead, she articulated much more clearly than I did. I identified myself and asked to see the owner, Joey Soong.

Her smile stiffened.

I gave her my most disarming smile. "I'm not a salesman. I'm a private investigator. I have a couple questions I think Mr. Soong can help me with."

Her smile still frozen, she replied, "I'll see if he's here." She disappeared into the rear through an open door, beyond which I saw several bustling Asians pushing laundry carts and hovering over various stainless steel vats from which bursts of steam gushed.

Moments later, she reappeared. "This way," she pointed to the aisle between rows of steaming vats in which I supposed laundry was being laundered. "His office is at the end of the aisle, on the right."

Joey Soong smiled up at me when I entered his office. If the décor of his office was any indication of the man, Joey Soong was spare, frugal, and no-nonsense. I discovered quickly his approach to business was more Western than Oriental.

"Please, have a seat." He gestured to a worn Captain's chair in front of his equally worn oak desk. A slight man, he wore a self-effacing smile on his slender face, but his eyes searched deep into mine. He extended his hand, "How can I help you, Mr. Boudreaux? I haven't done anything wrong, I hope."

"No," I laughed and shook his hand. "I appreciate your seeing me. I know you're busy."

"Yes, you know how it is. To quote Confucius, 'Time is money.'" I frowned, and he laughed. "Well, if he didn't say it, he should have."

I liked Joey Soong. He was nothing like I had expected. I cleared my throat, "I've been told you control the Sing Leon tong in Austin."

He shrugged. "*Control* is a strong word."

I hesitated, uncertain if there were some customs I needed to observe or if I should simply state what I wanted to learn. "Bear with me, please. I'm not familiar with your people's customs."

A crooked grin played over his face. "My people? I'm an American, Mr. Boudreaux."

My ears burned. With a self-conscious grin, I replied, "Maybe I should come straight to the point. It's just that—" I hesitated.

He finished my remark. "You just didn't know how to

handle Asians, right? That's what you were going to say?"

I laughed, "I suppose so."

He leaned forward and nodded. "Sure, many of the old folks cling to the habits of the old country, but most of us born in the good old U.S. of A. prefer to direct, no-nonsense approach to business. So, what can I do for you?"

"What's the difference between a tong and a triad?"

Joey Soong frowned. "Do you know someone in the triad?"

"No." I paused, wondering just how honest I should be with him and remembering Joe Ray, my insurance. "What can you tell me about some men by the names of Lei Sun Huang, Chang Yulan, and Lao Ning?"

The smile faded from his face. He eyed me suspiciously. "If you will excuse me for saying so, those are not good men to know, Mr. Boudreaux."

"I don't know them, but they are involved in a case I'm working on. So, tell me, what is the difference between tongs and triads?"

He shook his head. "Good and bad, Mr. Boudreaux. The Sing Leon tong in Austin is basically a fraternal—I suppose you could even say business—organization."

"Business?"

"Yes."

"I asked a cop friend of mine about the tong. He said it was sort of like the Chamber of Commerce. Members do business with members most of the time. Is that how it is?"

Joey nodded. "Not all tongs. There are some tongs that do have a criminal element," he paused. "But not in Austin. The only criminal element among the Asians in this city is the Ying On triad, and the three names you gave me are influential members of that triad."

"This traid you mentioned, the Ying On, what do they do?"

He shook his head. "Whatever they can—prostitution, bribery, auto theft, smuggling, just to name a few."

My ears perked up. "Smuggling? You mean drugs?"

"That too. Whatever the market will bear—arms, animals, snakes."

"Snakes?" I stared at him, a disbelieving smile flickering over my lips.

He nodded, "Whatever the market demands, Mr. Boudreaux." He hesitated. "We hear rumors of their activities. Nothing we can pin down. Two years ago, a young man named James Lu disappeared. James had grown up in our neighborhood. He was a member of the Ying On triad, and made the mistake of telling his brother the triad had just delivered two hundred thousand dollars worth of parrots to a pet dealer in Florida."

"Two hundred—" the words stuck in my throat. Finally, I managed to gasp out, "for parrots?"

With a terse nod, he explained, "Then there are the arms, and weapons, everything from infrared cameras to missile guidance systems. They bring in and ship out anything that is in demand."

I whistled softly, "What about the government? The FBI, or the local law?"

Joey arched an eyebrow and shook his head. "Any member of the triad who reveals any aspect of the organization ends up like James Lu." He paused, a look of sadness in his eyes. "Jimmy was my cousin and a good son to his parents. For some reason, he became involved with the Ying On. Like all criminal elements, once you're in, there's only one way out."

For several moments, I stared at Joey Soong, digesting the information he had given me however impalpable it might be. "What you're saying is there is no proof any of this is taking place?"

He nodded slowly. "I wish someone could come up with hard evidence. I'd like nothing better than to see the triad dismantled. The police have investigated, but have gained nothing. Talk to your friend, Joe Ray. He'll tell you."

I stiffened in surprise. "How do you know Joe Ray?"

Joey's eyes twinkled. "He called me and said you were coming over. He also said," he added, his dark eyes now laughing, "that if I didn't have you out within the hour, he was sending a cruiser."

All I could do was shake my head. I rose and offered him my hand. "I've made a fool of myself a lot, but this takes the cake."

He laughed out loud. "Forget it."

I grew serious. "One other name. I didn't mention it before, but now—well, what about Sam Bradford? Have you ever heard the name Samuel Bradford in conjunction with the Sing On triad?"

He shrugged. "Talk. Rumor."

"Nothing substantial, huh?"

"Nothing substantial."

Chapter Twenty-eight

As I drove away from Soong's Laundry, I glanced in the rearview mirror and spotted a light green car pull out and fall in behind me. I kept an eye on it until it turned off a few blocks down Seventh Street. What I didn't notice was the black one that turned off Walker onto Seventh and fell in behind me.

I turned south on the expressway and drove aimlessly. Five and a half days of pavement pounding and still nothing significant, nothing concrete. Of course, I knew now what had happened. While Albert Hastings might have been cavalier about the personal use of drugs, when he learned Lieutenant Governor-elect Bradford was involved in trafficking, he tried to dump him.

He must have had proof because he had given Landreth a sheath of documents, apparently backups to the originals. That explained why Hastings' office had been ransacked two days after his death, and why Landreth was murdered and his house torn apart just a few days ago.

But there was nothing concrete.

As much as I hated to admit it, I was at a dead-end.

I drove down to Zilker Park overlooking the green waters of the Colorado. I sat staring at the water churning downstream. Every lead had run up against a brick wall. Given time, I knew I could find the proof I needed, but the kicker was that I didn't have the time.

Proving a connection between Bradford and the smuggling was out of the question. Any evidence of the senator's involvement had been removed from Hastings' office. Even if I found the alleged documentation, there wasn't time to develop Bradford's complicity in Hastings' murder.

No, I told myself, starting the pickup and heading home. *The only chance left is to find Red Tompkins and hopefully the video.* And I warned myself I had as much chance of finding him as my old man had of giving up Thunderbird wine.

At the first signal light, a black Ford pulled up beside me, but I was too busy sorting through my thoughts to pay attention.

Red Tompkins. Red Tompkins.

I mulled over the story of his disappearance, hoping for inspiration, something I had missed, something I had overlooked.

Kwockwing Funeral Home was part of the Ying On triad. If Tompkins had proof that Packard was innocent, then Bradford had to get rid of him. *Why did Tompkins go to that particular funeral home?* Obviously because he recognized the alleged assassin.

How did Bradford know Tompkins had the video? The only persons the young man told of the incriminating tape were Danny's Uncle Liam and whomever he had recognized from the funeral home.

Nodding slowly, I mumbled, "When Tompkins went into the funeral home with word of the incriminating tape, someone inside had to contact either Bradford or Lei

Sun Huang for orders, and those orders were for the death of Red Tompkins.

So, how did they manage to get rid of the body?

Suddenly, I knew. I slammed the heel of my hand against my forehead. *That has to be the answer. It's got to be!*

Janice was waiting for me when I pulled into the drive. She had her own key, and she was watching TV when I opened the door. She glared at me. "Why didn't you call this morning? I wanted to go with you."

"You wouldn't believe it," I replied, going into detail about my old man.

When I finished, she asked, "So, you've got no idea where he is, huh?"

"Nope." With a shrug, I said, "I know it sounds loony on my part, but I was beginning to hope he'd changed."

She smiled sadly. "I'm sorry."

"Don't be. He just reinforced what I'd always thought. Right now, he could be anywhere. Dallas, San Antonio, or who knows? He could ring the doorbell at any time."

She rolled her eyes. "Yeah, you bet."

At that moment, the doorbell rang. Janice and I exchanged surprised looks. "No," she said, "it can't be."

I grunted. "Who knows? Nothing he does surprises me any longer." I opened the door expecting to see a frail bum in baggy clothes. Instead, I looked up into the chiseled features of Godzilla in a two-thousand-dollar Armani suit. It was Huey, Danny O'Banion's driver/bodyguard/ intimidator.

"Mr. O'Banion wants you should see him." He stepped aside, and I spotted Danny's sleek limo at the curb.

"Tony? Who is it?" she gasped when she saw Huey.

"You remember Huey from the barbecue. Danny wants to see me." I winked at her. "Why don't you entertain Huey while I see what Danny wants?"

She shot me a look filled with daggers, then craned her neck to stare up at Huey. "Would—would you care to come in, Mr. Huey?"

He shook his head and remained where he was.

I opened the car door and climbed in. "Danny."

He eyed me coolly, the ice in his eyes belying the faint smile on his face. "Hello, Tony. What news do you have for me?"

I settled back in the plush seat. "Not much, Danny."

"Still nothing?"

"Nothing firm. But I've got an idea."

He studied me. "Pretty late for ideas."

I ignored his sarcasm. "First, I can tell you who killed Hastings. It was a hit man from the Ying On triad. Put up to it by Sam Bradford who did not want Hastings to reveal the extent of his involvement with the triad and its smuggling activities, especially the drug trafficking."

Danny nodded, "I'd heard the smuggling rumors."

"Apparently, everyone has, but no one has been able to prove them."

He arched an eyebrow. "They ain't dummies, Tony."

I scooted around in the seat. "I can believe that. What I've found, I had to dig out with a pick and shovel. There isn't time to establish a chain of evidence linking Bradford to Hastings' murder. I see only one chance." I paused and shook my head once. "And not a good one at that, Danny."

He studied me a moment. When he spoke, his tone was reflective. "I knew there wasn't much of a chance when we lost the last appeal. At least this way, we're trying. What do you have in mind?"

"Red Tompkins."

"Red Tompkins? Who's he?"

"He's the Red who talked to your Uncle Liam. Tompkins mysteriously disappeared after entering the Kwockwing Funeral Home ten years ago."

"So?"

Shaking my head, I said. "I've got to hand it to those little Asian guys. They pull tricks that stagger the imagination."

Danny frowned, the freckles on his forehead bunching together. "You've lost me."

I leaned forward. "The only explanation for Tompkins' disappearance is that he was murdered in the funeral home and buried with one of the deceased." I released a deep breath and leaned back, staring at Danny.

After a moment, he said, "Are you sure, Tony? Real sure?"

"No. But it's all that's left." I frowned at him. "That's the only answer, Danny, the only possible answer."

He shook his head, doubt scribbled across his face.

"Listen, Danny. If we had time, we could find hard proof. There's always evidence. And evidence doesn't lie. Our problem is we don't have time." I paused and studied my old friend. "I'm no Sherlock Holmes, but I feel good about this. All I've got to do is identify those the funeral home buried that day."

He frowned. "What if nobody was buried?"

A shiver ran up my spine. "Don't even suggest that, Danny."

"Okay, so how do you go about finding out?"

I shrugged. "It's a piece of cake—obituaries, legal records. Don't worry; I can find out."

Leaning back in the seat, Danny nodded slowly. "There's something else you better find out."

"Yeah? What?" I frowned.

He pointed through the front windshield. "See that black Ford down there at the curb? They've been sitting there watching you."

Chapter Twenty-nine

I stood at the curb as Danny drove away. My gaze shifted to the black Ford down the street. Stepping off the curb I headed for the parked car, and as soon as I did it pulled away from the curb into a driveway, backed out, and disappeared in the opposite direction. A chill ran up my spine.

"What did he want?"

Janice's voice at my side startled me. "Huh? Oh, he was just wondering how the case was going."

She laid her hand on my arm. "It isn't going well, is it?"

I gave her a wry grin. "It could be better."

We lapsed into silence, staring down the deserted street thoughtfully. Finally, I drew a deep breath. I looked down at her, "Well, are you ready to play detective again?"

Her dark eyes twinkled. "What do you have in mind?"

Taking her elbow, I guided her back into my condo. "We don't have much time. First, let's see how far back the online archives of the *Austin Daily Press* go. Then I want to talk to Lorene Hastings."

"Albert Hastings' widow? Why?"

Everything I have is theory, but if I find what I want in

162

the archives, then she might provide me with the one final answer I'm looking for. Then I'll know my theory is right."

To my disappointment, the online archives for the Austin newspaper went back only eight years. That meant after I spoke with Lorene Hastings we would have to make a trip to the library.

When Lorene Hastings answered my call, I explained that I wanted permission to take a look at the executive lounge on the top floor of the Hastings' Building.

Though perplexed, she agreed, "Certainly, but what on earth for?"

Because of the taps on Landreth's phone, I was paranoid enough not to tell her over the phone that I wanted to make sure there was a window in the lounge—a window allowing the killer to escape. "I'm not certain, Mrs. Hastings. Just an idea, and it might prove to be nothing. Can you clear it for me?"

"Of course. Edmund Norville is the office manager. I'll call him."

"Thanks. I'll stop by later this afternoon."

"What was that for?" Janice asked when I punched off.

"Do you remember the video Floyd Holloman told us about?"

A puzzled frown wrinkled her forehead. "Do you mean the one Red carried in his boot heel?"

"Yes. Do you remember too that when the secretary entered the boardroom, she found only Hastings, dead? Right?"

"Right."

"That meant the killer had to have had another exit. A window in the executive lounge that opened onto a fire escape or something."

Janice considered my explanation. "What if there is no window or what if the killer hid until she left to call the police and then slipped out?"

I rolled my eyes. "I don't even want to think about that. If there is no window, it could be all over for Bobby Packard." *But,* I thought, *there has to be a window. Otherwise, how did the Asian hit man make his escape?*

"Where are we going now?"

"Now we head for the library, and if I find what I hope to find, then we'll head for Hastings' Real Estate."

The John Winston Public Library had none of the musty odor usually associated with libraries. Instead, its modern, cavernous rooms had the antiseptic smell of a hospital.

I led the way back to the archives.

Janice glanced up at me. "You've been here before, huh?" she spoke in hushed tones.

"It's my second home," I chuckled.

"Do you think it'll take long?"

"It shouldn't. According to Floyd Holloman, Tompkins disappeared October 3."

"The day before Hollomon's wife's birthday," Janice smiled.

"You remember, huh?"

"That's hard to forget."

"Anyway, we'll start at October 1. Look through the obits until we find whoever was buried by Kwockwing Funeral Home on the third."

"And then . . . ?"

Without breaking stride, I replied, "And then we dig them up."

Janice jerked to a halt. "We what?" Her voice carried, causing several patrons to look up. She pressed her fingers to her lips, and gasped in disbelief, "We what?"

I gestured for her to follow me. "We dig them up," I whispered. "How else am I going to find the tape?"

She gurgled in disbelief once or twice, then hurried after me.

We entered a large room containing a dozen microfiche readers that looked like computers with an anemic keyboards and monitors overdosed on steroids. "Go on over there. I'll get the microfiche."

Swapping my driver's license for the October, 1994, *Austin Daily Press* microfiche, I returned to Janice and inserted it into the reader.

October 1 obits listed seventeen deaths. Only one was serviced at Kwockwing Funeral Home, a Robert L. Hsu. Burial was at the Golden Threads Cemetery. The next day's obituaries listed two more, Lau Gai Chin and Joseph N. Lam, both interred at Queen's Park Cemetery.

All three interments were scheduled October 3, 1994.

I crossed my fingers.

Red Tompkins had to be in one of those graves.

Our first stop was the local drug store where I purchased a throwaway camera. Our next stop was Queen's Park, one of the oldest cemeteries in Austin. As we pulled through the main gates and headed for the office, Janice glanced out the rear window. "It's peaceful out here," she said softly.

I suppressed a wisecrack. "Yeah."

The main office was a solemn red brick structure smothered with English ivy. Inside, a plump woman in her mid-forties or so greeted us with the bright smile of an accomplished salesperson.

Glibly, I explained that my wife and I were passing through from San Francisco. Some of our neighbors asked us to snap some pictures of their relatives' graves.

The smile on her face flickered, then held despite no hope for a sale. "Here are their names," I said, handing her the sheet of paper. "If you could tell us the plot number and point us in the right direction, we'd be most grateful."

"Certainly," she replied, slipping in front of the computer. She looked up in surprise. "These are Chinese names."

Janice smiled sweetly, "Yes, our neighbors are Chinese."

I grinned at her. She was learning to lie with the best of us.

"Certainly, certainly," the saleswoman replied, hastily typing in the names. "They'll be in the Chinese Cemetery," she said over her shoulder. "Straight down the drive out front and right on Oriental Lane." She hit the print button and leaned back while the laser printer spat out two sheets of paper.

She scanned them, then looked up at me. "You did say Lau Gai Chin and Joseph N. Lam?"

I cut my eyes to the two sheets in her hand. "Yes. Is something wrong?"

"Oh, no. Not at all," she handed me the two pages. "It's just that they were both cremated."

Cremated! I maintained my composure. "I understand."

She added, "Their ashes are contained in the sealed urns which are part of their headstones."

Back in the Silverado, Janice lifted her eyebrows. "Now what? If Tompkins was in either of those caskets, whatever he had is ashes now."

Shaken by the news, I nodded down the drive. "Let's keep up the pretext anyway. We said we wanted pictures, let's get pictures."

All of the headstones in the Chinese Cemetery faced east, which I figured was part of a tradition. We were lucky to have the row and plot number since the headstones were written in the traditional Chinese characters.

Each of the graves had a funerary burner nearby, a brick oven that served as a safe place for the ritualized burning of spiritual tributes to the dead.

I snapped a couple pictures while Janice remained in the truck. When I climbed back in, she nodded across the cemetery. "Maybe I'm getting paranoid, Tony, but do you see that tan car over there." She nodded across rows of headstones to a small Honda a couple hundred yards away.

"What about it?"

"It might be nothing, but they followed us into the cemetery. They've just been sitting over there. Do you think—" She hesitated, grimaced, then shrugged. "I'm just jittery. I guess it's being out here, you know, with dead people and all."

I didn't laugh. "Probably visiting family or idle curiosity. Some people get kicks out of reading headstones." I shifted into gear. "Still," I added, "let's keep watch."

Chapter Thirty

As we pulled out of the cemetery onto the street, Janice exclaimed, "The car's following us, Tony!"

I drove below the speed limit. "Just keep watching."

Two blocks later, I turned right. Janice caught her breath when the small car followed.

Keeping my eyes on the rearview mirror, I held my speed. Finally, the Honda turned left. Janice sighed with relief, "He's gone. I guess it was just my imagination."

"Maybe, but we'd be smart to keep a sharp eye."

We rode in silence for a few minutes, winding through the late afternoon traffic across town to the Golden Threads Cemetery.

"What if this one has been cremated too?"

I gripped the steering wheel tightly. "Then it's over for Bobby Packard."

"Is that something traditional about the Chinese? I mean, cremation?"

"I have no idea," I said remembering what Joey Soong had told me. "It might be among the older generation but the person I know is just like us." I hesitated and grinned crookedly at her. "Well, like me . . . not like you little rich girls."

She pouted her lips and slapped playfully at my shoulder. "You know better than that."

Despite the palpable apprehension in the cab of the pickup, we both laughed.

Golden Threads spread over rolling hills lush with grass, flowering bushes, and stately trees. I went inside the office while Janice remained in the pickup, her eyes fixed on the road leading into the cemetery.

I used the same pretext at Golden Threads, and the salesman was just as helpful. Ten minutes later, we were snapping pictures of the weathered headstone of Robert L. Hsu at Row H, plot E10. The traditional funerary burner, this one shaped like a miniature pagoda, sat next to the headstone.

To my delight, the grave was within a hundred feet of the tall privet hedge around the perimeter of the cemetery. "Things look good," I muttered, smiling down at Janice. "Now, let's see if there is a window in the executive lounge at Hastings'."

During the drive to the Hastings' Real Estate Building, I kept a close eye on the rearview mirror. *Were we being followed?* I couldn't tell. I'd pick out a vehicle, and moments later it turned off. I finally decided I was becoming too suspicious for my own good.

We parked outside the ten-story red brick building. I looked up. My pulse raced. There was a fire escape on the north side of the building. I crossed my fingers. "I'll be right back."

Janice smiled. "Good luck." She held up crossed fingers.

I took the elevator to the top floor. A matronly receptionist looked up at me quizzically, "Yes, sir?"

I identified myself. "Mrs. Hastings was to tell Mr. Norville I was on the way over."

Her eyes lit with wary recognition as her lips twisted in distaste. "Oh, yes. Something about the executive lounge."

"Yes, Ma'am. It'll only take a moment."

She indicated a set of double doors to her right. "It's right through there. The lounge is the first door on the left. I unlocked it for you."

As soon as I opened the lounge door, I spotted the window. Though it was opaque, I spotted a shadow beyond. I crossed my fingers, hoping the shadow was the fire escape.

Throwing open the window, I wanted to shout.

There it was, in all its glory. The fire escape, the route the killer had used to leave the building.

Back in the pickup, I grinned at Janice. "Believe it or not, a piece of my theory just proved true."

"Would you look at that," I muttered as we turned onto Payton Gin Road just down the street from my apartment.

"I don't believe it," Janice said when she spotted my old man sitting in the midst of cigarette butts and empty beer cans on the front porch. In one hand he held a can of Old Milwaukee and in the other a Camel cigarette.

"I told you," I said, shaking my head as I turned into the drive. "Nothing he does surprises me any more."

"Good afternoon, Mr. Boudreaux," Janice said brightly as she climbed out of the pickup.

My greeting wasn't as pleasant. "Where did you disappear to this morning?"

He shrugged and took a drag off his cigarette. "Friends," he replied in a raspy voice, his eyes fixed on the street in front of us, "I got friends. You don't got to worry none."

Angered by his obvious indifference for any concern over him, I stared down at him, at a complete loss for words. I clenched my teeth.

Janice tugged at me. "Let's go inside and see what we can whip up for dinner."

Once inside, I growled, "I don't know if I can stand him until Thanksgiving."

She laughed brightly. "Sure you can. Now, how do we go about tonight?"

"I thought you were hungry."

Glancing briefly at the front door, she replied, "I just wanted to get you inside. I could see you were getting angry. But now that you mention it," she added, "I *am* hungry. What do you have to eat around here?" She opened the refrigerator and whistled. "Do you think you bought enough beer for your father?"

"I haven't bought him any beer since that case Saturday night."

She opened the door wide, inviting me to take a look. "Someone has."

The shelves were stacked with cans of Old Milwaukee— enough to last the average tippler a month, but my old man, probably two days. "Someone certainly has!" I glanced around the kitchen, but all the appliances were in their places. I couldn't help wondering where he had found the money for beer.

Janice opened the small chest freezer next to the refrigerator and rummaged through the TV dinners. "Let's see. We have a broad choice of fried chicken, chicken nuggets, sliced chicken, or lemon chicken," she announced, staring into the condensation billowing from the open door.

"How about the lemon chicken," I replied, closing the refrigerator door. "I feel like something exotic tonight." I winked at her. "In fact, if I had some Thunderbird wine, we could have it with the chicken."

She shivered at the thought of cheap wine. "Sorry, but you'll have to make do with hot coffee." She pulled out a third dinner. "I'll prepare one for your father. He might be hungry, too."

I snorted. "With all that beer? I doubt it." I reached for the telephone. "I'll call Jack while you nuke the dinners."

"Jack? Edney?"

"For tonight. When we start digging, I want to dig fast."

She closed the oven door. "But, I can help you dig."

"I mean to dig fast. I doubt if there is any security out there, but we could run into some parked teenagers or who knows, even some vampires," I said, baring my teeth.

I arranged to meet Jack at the corner of Jain Lane and Perry, four blocks from Golden Threads Cemetery, at 1:00 A.M. "I need help, Jack," I explained. "I'll tell you more, but if you help me on this, I'll run your campaign for city council."

He jumped at the offer. "Can I bring Diane?"

"No."

John Roney preferred Old Milwaukee to a chicken dinner. After a couple bites of lemon chicken, I thought maybe he had made the wiser choice. On the other hand, had I taken a beer, I would have been saddled with guilt.

I stepped out onto the porch where he was dutifully knocking down another Old Milwaukee. "Who bought the beer?"

His words were slurred. "I told you. I got friends."

"What're their names?"

He shook his head. "I got them. Don't worry." His reply was testy, defensive.

"Do I know them?"

"A big guy took me to get beer and then brought me here. Like I said, I got friends."

"Black car?"

My old man nodded and blew out a stream of smoke.

A big guy. It had to be Huey. "Thanks, Danny," I whispered under my breath.

Chapter Thirty-one

Jack Edney was waiting in the parking lot of an all-night Wal-Mart when we drove up beside him. "Climb in. We only need one vehicle."

"What are we going to do?" He looked around the parking lot. "Turn over outhouses?" he chuckled.

"Get in. I'll tell you."

He spotted the two shovels in the pickup bed. He greeted Janice as he slammed the door and asked, "What are the shovels for?"

I shifted into gear and headed for the cemetery. "Old friend, you and I are going to dig up a grave."

"We're what?" he stared at me in disbelief, a half smile on his face as if I were setting him up for a joke.

"You heard me right—a grave."

He frowned at Janice. "Is this idiot serious?"

Janice nodded. "He's serious as can be."

Jack leaned back in the seat, folded his arms across his chest, and shook his head adamantly. "Take me back. I'm not digging up any grave. Not for you or anybody else."

"You've got to, Jack. You're the only one I can trust."

He snorted. "Hey, boy. I've got breaking news for you. You can't trust me either. What if we get caught? The publicity could ruin my chances for Austin City Council."

"We won't get caught. We'll park in the street. There's a large hedge around the cemetery and a grove of trees around the grave. You could hide an army in there."

"No." He stared straight ahead.

"I told you I'd run your campaign for you. What else do you want?"

"I want to go back to my Cadillac. Besides, if we're caught, there won't be a campaign."

I played my trump card. "You really owe me, Jack."

He chortled. "Oh? And just what makes you say that?"

I pulled over to the curb across the street from the dark cemetery. Traffic was light at 1:00 in the morning. Sensible people were home in bed. "Remember Vicksburg? I got you that additional four or five million in your inheritance."

He shot me a blistering look. "You're never going to let me forget that, are you?"

With nonchalant aplomb, I shrugged. "Probably not."

Then he began to whine, "All right, Tony. So I owe you for that, but a cemetery? At night? What if—well—"

I put as much sarcasm as I could in my voice. "Surely you don't believe in ghosts or anything like that?"

He glanced tentatively at Janice, then straightened his shoulders. "Of course not. No one does."

"Then let's go," I said, tossing him a pair of leather gloves and opening the door. "Grab a shovel."

Moments later, we pushed through the hedge and hurried across three rows to Row H, plot E10, the resting place of Robert L. Hsu.

Janice held the flashlight beam on the center of the grave.

"If my reputation is going to be ruined," Jack whispered as we started digging. "I think I'm entitled to know what it's going to be ruined for."

I sunk the blade deep in the ground. "I think so too, Jack. A man's life depends on what we find here."

"Huh?" He paused and looked around at me.

"Dig," I growled, already feeling the sweat rolling down my spine and ribs.

In a soft voice, Janice took over the explanation. "We think two men are buried in this grave."

Jack stopped again. "Two?"

"Dig, Jack," I muttered a soft curse, "just dig." We were already a couple feet down.

"Anyway," Janice whispered, continuing, "if we're right, one of them has a videotape in the heel of his boot."

"And the tape," I put in, "identifies who really killed Albert Hastings."

Beyond the hedge, a passing car honked.

Jack jumped, startled.

"Just a car horn. Keep digging."

We both lapsed into silence. Our breathing grew ragged, but we continued until the blade of Jack's shovel struck metal.

"That's it," I whispered. "Hop out, Jack. I'll finish it up."

"Gladly," he mumbled, throwing a knee over the lip of the grave and rolling out. "You're not going to get me fooling around with a stiff, especially one that's been dead all these years."

I wasn't any too anxious either.

Frantically, I heaved another dozen or so shovels of soil from the grave, then dropped to my knees and brushed the dirt from the foot of the casket. "Shine the light down here," I whispered, "so I can find a latch of some sort."

The yellow beam played along the edge of the silver casket.

"Here they are." There was a latch at the end and one on the side. I sat back on my haunches and drew several deep breaths while tying my handkerchief over my nose.

I looked up. "Ready?"

The peripheral glow of the flashlight illuminated the frown on Janice's face. She whispered, "What if we're wrong, Tony?"

Setting my jaw, I glared at the casket. I clenched my teeth. "We aren't."

"Well, somebody do something, and let's get out of here," Jack growled.

Leaning forward, I popped the latches free. I grabbed the lip of the top, then hesitated. *What if I had indeed guessed wrong? But no. I couldn't have. This was the only logical explanation for the disappearance of Red Tompkins.* I closed my eyes and muttered a very short but even more sincere prayer.

"Come on, Tony. Raise the lid," Jack insisted anxiously. "Get it done and let's get out of here.

At first, the lid resisted, and then it swung open.

The bright beam of the flashlight lit up the end of the casket, revealing two pairs of feet, one in cloth sandals, the other, in cowboy boots.

Excitement pounded in my skull, and I barely heard Janice exclaiming, "There it is, Tony. There it is! Hurry! Try the heel."

I held my breath against the odor. Hastily, I grabbed a boot and fumbled for the heel. I twisted at it, but it refused to budge. My ears were pounding from holding my breath. I sucked in a lungful of air and gagged.

"Try the other one," Janice said. "Hurry."

I leaned forward and grabbed the other boot and twisted

the heel. It didn't budge. I tried harder, and this time, to my surprise, the heel rotated and a small aluminum canister fell out. Hastily, I grabbed it and worked off the top.

Curled neatly inside was a roll of videotape.

I grinned up at Janice and Jack. "We've got it."

A gutteral voice broke the darkness as did the beam of two flashlights. "Your mistake, Mr. Boudreaux. *We've* got it."

Chapter Thirty-two

I froze, the small canister clutched in one hand, the top in the other.

The second voice spoke with the singsong of an Asian accent. "Put the top back on the container and throw it up here."

My brain raced. I played for time. We didn't have much of a chance, but you never knew what would happen until you made the effort. I tried to come up with some ploy to distract them. Then I had an idea—a crazy one, but our only chance.

Rising to my feet, I dropped my arm to my side and eased it slightly behind my back. "Who are you?" At the same time, I turned the open canister upside down and felt the tape fall into the palm of my hand.

"That isn't important. What is important is the video-tape. Now throw it out, or we'll take it off you after you're dead."

I made an elaborate show of replacing the top while palming the tape. I held the canister up in one hand, hoping to distract them while I slipped the tape into my pocket with my other hand. "Here it is." Abruptly, I lobbed the canister into the darkness over Janice's head.

"Hey, what—" Both goons jerked around. I leaped for the feet of the one nearest me. "Grab the other one, Jack."

My sudden attack knocked my assailant's feet from under him. I scrambled to my knees and leaped forward. Next moment, my head exploded into a thousand stars. I was barely aware of someone cursing me and kicking me in the belly.

I struggled toward awareness, knowing I probably had only seconds to live.

Then other voices broke into the jumbled thoughts in my head. The kicking stopped. Hands pulled me to my feet. Then Janice was beside me. "Tony, Tony, are you all right? Did they hurt you?"

I blinked several times. Slowly several fuzzy figures outlined by bright beams came into focus. In the glow of the lights I saw a half dozen grim-faced Asians holding assault weapons on two others.

One of the more slight Asians nodded to me and shined his flashlight toward the hedge. There in the beam of the bright light stood Huey. "Go now," the Asian said.

Danny was parked behind my pickup. Huey opened the rear door of the limo. "Climb in," Danny said, "and give me your keys. One of my boys will take that piece of junk you drive back to your place. Do you have the tape?"

I patted my pocket.

"Good." He cut his eyes to Jack. "Get in and close the door. I want to see the tape."

I wanted to see it too, but I also wanted to know how he managed to pull our bacon from the fire.

"Thank Joey Soong. He put a tail on you when you left his laundry." Danny laughed. "He said you were pretty slick. He had to use a dozen cars to keep up with you. The black one we saw at your place belonged to him."

"Those were his boys back there?"

I wasn't surprised when Danny didn't give me a straight answer. "I told you, Tony. My bosses work with them. I couldn't afford to mix up in it."

Back at Danny's office, we viewed the video. As Red Tompkins had claimed, the tape caught Bobby Packard as he left the office. Moments later, a squat Asian entered the office, fired three shots into Hastings, and disappeared into the executive lounge, but not before turning to face the camera as if he were auditioning for a part in a movie.

"Well, well, well," Danny mumbled when he saw the face of the assassin, "if it isn't a young Lao Ning."

I looked around at him in surprise. "You know him?"

"He's an important man in the hierarchy of the Ying On triad. Years back, he was one of their hit men. Then he graduated." Danny grinned at me. "Well, old buddy, you done good, once again. I'll make copies of this, one of which will inexplicably show up on the Governor's breakfast table in—" he hesitated, glanced at his watch, then said, "four hours."

"What about the mess back at the cemetery? I'd planned to fill the grave back in so the cops wouldn't get involved."

Danny's grin grew wider. "It's all taken care of, the two goons included. When the sun comes up, no one will know the cemetery had any visitors at all last night. As far as you're concerned, you two were out dancing all evening. I'll take it from there."

"How are you going to explain the tape?"

His Tom Sawyer grin spread over his freckled face. "It just showed up in the mail. Probably from some poor soul with a guilty conscience."

I stared at him in disbelief, but knowing Danny, that explanation would probably go unquestioned. "What about those two goons back there?"

His grin faded. "You don't want to know."

"How do we go about taking care of Bradford and the others now?"

"Lei Sun Huang? Chang Yu-lan?" he shook his head. "They're history. Their own kind will take care of them once this tape is made public." He paused and added, "Don't worry. Everything's taken care of."

Janice shook her head. "I still can't believe it about Sam Bradford."

Danny smiled at her. "Try not to think about it." He looked around. "Huey, take them home." He winked at us. "You two check your social calendars. When my little cousin comes home, he'll be by to thank you, so you might as well expect one wingding of a party."

"We'll be ready," I said, winking back at him.

As I reached the office door, Danny stopped me. "By the way, Tony. Your old man is gone. After you left tonight, he caught a freight for Dallas."

His words cut into my heart like a knife. I guess I had my hopes too high, and I should have known better. Still, I drew a deep breath and, releasing it slowly, grinned weakly at Janice and while shrugging in resignation at Danny. "Well, at least I'm batting five hundred. Saved one and lost one. Maybe next time it'll all work out."

"Next time," Jack Edney said as we rode the elevator down to the parking lot, "is when you help me win the election. You know, Tony, I've been thinking. Maybe you could use an assistant campaign manager."

"Oh?" I had a sinking feeling. I hated to ask the next question, "Who did you have in mind?"

"Diane. I think she would be an asset, don't you?"

All I could do was close my eyes and fall back against the elevator wall.

Laying her head on my shoulder, Janice said in a silky

smooth voice with a touch of amusement. "Cheer up, Tony. It'll be fun. I'll help you. Besides, I've decided that I like this business, and I want to work with you on your next case."

The elevator wall was all that kept me from collapsing.